THE BRUSSELS REVIEW

Spring 2026

Web ISSN 3041-4431
Print ISSN 3041-4423
ISBN 978-2-39069-060-3

thebrusselsreview.com
shop.thebrusselsreview.com
info@thebrusselsreview.com
marketing@thebrusselsreview.com

Featured artist:

Vlada Teaca is a photographer working between Brussels and Berlin. Born in Moldova, she left home at nineteen and moved through several European cities while refining her photographic practice and shaping her artistic voice. Now based in Berlin, she focuses on conceptual and surrealist portraiture, exploring the delicate border between reality and dreams.

Instagram: @ vlada_tc

CONTENT

NONFICTION

POETRY

FICTION

PREFACE

Grief. Reminiscence. Trauma. Watermelons. This collection of stories is bound together by complex and varied approaches to human emotion and how we react to change in our lives. Breakups, the deaths of loved ones, new homes, and pasts we cannot leave behind. Each of our authors tackles one of these topics through their own unique lens, offering gripping narratives and meaningful writing that invite readers to immerse themselves in the words on the pages beyond.

FICTION

Jacqueline Chou's "An Ode to Jammie Evans" delivers a poignant memoir of 1970s childhood poverty, racial taunts, and the redemptive kindness of a classmate scapegoated for a stolen quarter pile. It circles back decades later to a taqueria reunion, where quiet decency confronts lingering guilt. The story becomes a belated hymn of gratitude and guilt, charting how adult self-knowledge is forged in the long aftershock of a single misdirected punishment and a long-overdue apology.

Marcus Delmont's "Three Days" is a quiet, short piece about compassion and humanity in the face of difference. Throughout the titular "three days," it demonstrates how understanding and common ground can be forged despite cultural and linguistic differences. An important, timeless narrative that will remain relevant for years to come.

Meryl Franzos's "Hair of the Dog" is a moving story of a woman's traumatic experience from the past resurfacing to haunt her in the present. Through the thematic complexity of the narrative, Franzos establishes a character who struggles between her inner sense of morality and her personal obligation to exact justice.

A marriage between narrative and execution that reveals why grammatical choices are just as important as the story itself, Erin

Gaura's "Bed Linens" demonstrates how overwriting can, in the right context, become a tool for enriching a story's themes. The syntax is beautifully overdetailed and hyperfixated on the unimportant, relatably reflecting how one's mind becomes overstimulated in the emotional aftermath of a breakup.

In Kevin MacAlan's "Wish You Were Here," filial grief curdles into denial as a son, unable to face his father's death, fabricates a West Indies cricket odyssey through forged postcards and torn-away stamps. The narrative patiently dismantles his fantasy, revealing how language, paperwork, and office protocol conspire to force him back into the difficult work of mourning and rejoining the world of the living.

Scott Macmann's "A Child's Christmas in Ohio" is a tale of friendship, adventure, and the sobering reality of negligent parenting told through the lens of child innocence. With "Gracie," the author focuses on the intricacies of adult relationships as a married couple struggles with the tragedy of their beloved cat's imminent demise. Through both of his works, Macmann manages to create a relatable yet heartbreaking narrative with a profound emotional effect on the reader.

In "The People's Choice," John Picard demonstrates his unique narrative versatility. His ability to showcase the gut-wrenching realities of a veteran struggling with PTSD alongside the falsities of a reality star's glamorous life produces a compelling dynamic of nightmare-fueled existence and compassion from unexpected places.

An absurdist take on coping mechanisms, anticonsumerism, and science versus nature debates, Anthony Schneck's "Flavor Profile" is told through one person's quest to prove that watermelons have subtly changed their taste. With such a wide range of themes, it is a story that asks for attentive close reading and will, doubtless, provide each consumer with a unique literary "flavor profile" of their own.

Set on a Cambridgeshire building site in 1988, Thomas Wright's "Anglo-Irish," probes generational rifts among Irish immigrants and racism through a teen skivvy's summer with his uncle Stephen's crew, before university beckons. It meditates on cultural identity forged in cement dust, passive-smoking, and the grandmother's rosary beads across emigrant lines.

NONFICTION

Mark D. Crimmins's "Glimpses of Gangnam" is an exercise in stream of consciousness, born from sitting in a busy, ostensibly uneventful café in Seoul's most conspicuous district, sipping drinks, eating cake, and thinking on the page. Stories emerge from moments, small, occasionally inconsequential happenings that, when paused, seen, and perhaps elevated with some thrills or chills, open up space for reflection and give shape to meaning.

As a real American author, fascinated by words and their poetics, James B. Nicola finds reason on gender gaps through the Romance Languages. In his "The Gentle Revolution," he shares his remarks with generosity, proving how language, when closely observed, can signal respect and arouse parity and progress.

Ann Perrins's "Asparagus, a Gift for Audrey" is that delightful read one wants for company on a Sunday afternoon by a sun-bathed bay window. With a nostalgic smile, the writer meets the reader halfway through the streets of a quiet British village. There, in a past time with details only a fresh memory can deliver, we enjoy the evidence of a bond between two women, whom culture might have kept apart but shared love has brought together.

Pete Warzel's "Damage" springs from a near-disastrous car incident in his neighborhood. With remarkable attention to the emotions at stake, Pete maps a first-hand experience with words apt for recreating the scene as if it were happening now. The story not only renders one's unraveling thoughts during danger but tackles the implications of our actions and their lasting imprint on those in near proximity.

POETRY

In this issue's poetry, compression becomes revelation. The lyric voice distills grief, endurance, irony, and private reckoning into concentrated moments that linger long after the page is turned.

Collin Garrity's poems confront the modern landscape with wry intelligence and moral unease. In works such as "Leafblower" and "Hospital Poem," the everyday object becomes an instrument of existential inquiry; lawns, tools, and clinical spaces expose the quiet absurdities and fragilities of contemporary life.

Olivia Soule's "The Deep End of the Pool" moves through mythic invocation and personal vulnerability with incantatory repetition. Her language circles loss and inheritance, invoking Poseidon and Midas while remaining grounded in bodily experience and grief.

Ann Marie Gamble offers poems that are at once intimate and philosophically alert. In "Just Asking" and "Trying," she balances tenderness with clarity, confronting aging, inevitability, and filial love without sentimentality.

Ty Cronkhite's work demonstrates formal versatility and tonal control. In "Ode to the Ellipses," punctuation becomes metaphor, a meditation on absence, implication, and the unfinished thought. In "Sonnet Regarding Buttons," he adopts a traditional form to explore emotional volatility with wit and structural precision, reminding us that classical architecture can still contain modern anxiety.

Together, these poets demonstrate that brevity need not diminish depth. Their work inhabits the charged space between thought and feeling, where language—pared down and sharpened—becomes both witness and measure of what it means to endure.

MARK CRIMMINS

Glimpses Of Gangnam

It's 7:35 PM and you have a perfect seat here at this cafe in Gangnam, just back from the main road and right across the street from a parked white Bentley with tinted windows. Next to the Bentley is a cheaper but spiffy white car with dark windows and stroboscopic wheels. Across the curved intersection, a tower of clubs and restaurants rises into the night. Room of Soju is up there on the fourth floor. MTL Modern Bar is on the second. Tri Land (Cocktails, Beer, Wine, Whisky) also occupies a spot on the second floor. The Shuffle Pub is on the eighth floor and calls itself a lounge bar.

You are sat by a window at street level and thus you are exposed to whoever walks past. You are hardly invisible, but you appear to be working on your computer, so perhaps you won't attract any attention. You are having a strawberry juice and a cup of ice.

A silver van, faded and dirty, pulls up right behind the white Bentley. The van's driver gets out and looks angrily at the Bentley. He is a young guy in a baseball cap and seems to be making a delivery of some kind. As though he will now proceed to box the Bentley's ears, he puts on gloves.

You are sipping your strawberry juice in its cup of ice. You can only sip because the pieces of ice are so small that the drink has developed what could only be called a technical flaw: the ice is so fine that it will

* *Mark Crimmins is a writer and Associate Professor of English Studies at the Chinese University of Hong Kong, Shenzhen. He previously taught at the University of Toronto (1999–2016). He holds an MA (1993) and a PhD (1999) in Twentieth Century Literature from the University of Toronto. Born in Manchester, England, he has lived in the United Kingdom, the United States, Japan, Canada, and China. His fiction has been published internationally since 2010. https://www.markcrimmins.com/*

only allow you to swig a little juice each time you imbibe.

A smart family (mom, pop, and girl of ten) stops at the Bentley as though to get into it. The owners, after all, could just be shoppers. But no! They walk on. The stupendous white machine is not theirs.

You try to get some of that strawberry juice down, and it is still not easy.

On a high floor of the flashy building across from you is Cube Music Town, its tantalizing advertisement reminding you it is still early in Gangnam: "Open pm 5.00/Close am 10.00." It is what you call Jumbo Jet Time—7:47 PM. Perhaps Gangnam's denizens have not yet got out of bed after their Thursday night romps.

Across from you and behind the Bentley is a large sculpture of an inflated figure. Similar inflated stickmen-like figures often flanked concert stages in the past. The inflated figures would flop over or stiffen as blasts of inflationary air blew through them.

The headlights of the Bentley lit up! It is chauffeur driven, perhaps.

The coffee shop is almost empty, and you have a perfect position. There are thirteen tables on the ground floor, but only three of them are occupied. You have jiggled your table around so that you have a wall at your back.

Three girls are sitting behind you talking in loud bursts of Hangul. One of them has a huge brightly colored hair curler rolled onto the top of her head. You are wondering if she is fixing her hair right there or if this plastic roller—arrested at the top of the head of an otherwise well-dressed girl—is a sort of Gangnam fashion. Facing you are two other young women conversing with loud voices.

A few people enter the coffee shop, most of them going upstairs. You too went upstairs, but you couldn't get the money seat by the window, so you retreated down here.

Right next to the glass as you are, you feel like a vulnerable target. Anyone could approach the window, press themselves against it, stick their tongues out, perhaps bang the glass, as visitors sometimes bash the gorilla compound windows in zoos.

However, nobody does this.

The Bentley's headlights are still on, but the car has yet to move.

Behind it, the figure, concrete and painted white, stands about four stories high. The legs are apart, and the right hand is held up towards the sky with his middle finger extended. Is he flipping the bird at the world or pointing to something in the sky? Perhaps even a crude gesture can be construed as a sign of transcendence.

Like many human-form statues in Seoul, the figure has no features, no face.

A fully loaded black Mustang with tinted windows turns the corner and drives past. A low-slung electric blue BMW parks between your window and Tom n Toms Coffee.

"You are more than beautiful," a clothing store sign across the street assures you.

Suddenly, an astonishing sight! Weaving gracefully around the intersection's bent S, an attractive girl in a trench coat, dolled to the nines, hair flowing behind her, rides a tiny motorized scooter, a sort of contraption, with an improvised seat attached to it. The girl glides past the window like a fashionista Valkyrie in a Sesame Street sketch. A rider on the storm. A dazzling witch straddling a modified space junk scooter.

The cafe is now filling up. A woman in a mini dress and ankle boots, a shawl around her shoulders. Two girls with a cake box. A young guy in a sweatshirt and jeans. Two men, businessmen, take a corner table. And, next to you, a sort of ritzy couple. The man goes out to have a smoke, stands across the street and watches through the glass as you look at his wife, who sits across from you. She has her compact out and is powdering her face. The girl in the mini dress seems to be with them. Could she be their daughter?

All the customers in the coffee shop suddenly speak loudly; their voices create a cacophony.

The smoker comes back in and takes his seat just beyond your laptop screen. You worry that he will bump your table and knock your drink onto your keyboard. But he manages not to.

Outside, a youth walks past, his shoulder bag bearing a message: "Replace Fear With Curiosity." This seems like sage and timely advice for the writer of these words.

The Bentley's headlights are still on. It seems as though the vehicle's departure is imminent. Or could someone have triggered the beams by passing too close to the car?

A mother escorts her tiny daughter past the window. The little girl, her dainty feet in miniature pink pumps, propels herself along on a hip little scooter.

"This too is Gangnam," you think.

The two girls across from you look at their phone screens and make selfie faces. Well, they are hardly the only two people in the world doing that, are they? The selfie epidemic—it's just another manifestation of this Age of Narcissism.

The wife of the man at the table in front of you (or the woman you think is his wife,) is obsessively looking out of the window. Perhaps the young guy is with the girl in the mini dress. Maybe she isn't the couple's daughter after all.

You become peckish, probably because of the speed at which you type. Thirteen hundred words have appeared on your screen since you took a seat here and started to type. You buy a large blob of tiramisu and a big Americano. Fuel, Gangnam-style. This creates a minor logistical challenge for your cramped tabletop. You remove the cake's wrapper and put it under the golden tray the cake rests on, between it and the plate.

A black-windowed BMW 7-Series rolls slowly across your view.

You take both of your trays to the serving station to get rid of them. Your phone is neatly placed on your red Moleskine notebook, the one in which you have been scribbling, indecisively, Cityscape Seoul or Seoul à la Carte. The notebook's soft cover means each page is earthquaked by the weight of your writing hand and the pressure of the pen. You have had many chances to regret choosing a soft-covered Moleskine in a rush as you sped through Terminal 2 of the Hong Kong Airport, late for your Seoul flight.

After making a funny face at the man and the woman, the mini dress girl from the next table goes outside for a smoke and stands just on the other side of the window from you. You are still trying to decide if the man and woman are husband and wife. The mini dress girl is wearing the ankle boots that are very much de rigueur in the Seoul of 2017.

Around the corner rumbles a blinged-out, jacked-up, enormous black Mini, which almost flattens the mini-dressed girl smoking outside. A burly man gets out of the car, handing it over to a couple of well-dressed young women who emerge from a nearby building, climb inside, and drive off. Perhaps the car belonged to one of the women, and the burly man was the valet.

The smoking girl, as though in fear, hurries back inside.

The man next to you has waltzed across the street to have another smoke between the Bentley and the spiffy white car with the dark windows. A young couple has joined the three people next to you and the gang is now seriously crowding your space. You fear they might ask you to move or change tables, something you are not willing to do. You like having this wall at your back and have a perfect typing position—you're not going to give it up easily. If their group is now complete, perhaps they will all relocate to one of Gangnam's clubs: Room of Soju or the Shuffle Pub.

The gang squeezes around the table beside you. Soon, with a chorus of laughs, they leave. Your guess was right. Your writing spot is no longer under threat. You move the unoccupied table a foot to the right to give yourself elbow room.

Your tiramisu is Gangnam tiramisu: huge and flashy but not really that great.

Two cars with dark windows crawl around the corner and ooze away. The Bentley has just driven off. Nobody ever did get into or out of it. A tinted Aston Martin appears. Souped up, it revs like a hot rod. A white VW SUV takes the place vacated by the Bentley on the curved corner in front of the massive sculpture flipping the bird at the heavens. You notice the white figure has an illuminated white heart.

An elongated black Maserati with tinted windows drives past the window, its headlights illuminating what looks like snow but is just a strangely brief downpour.

People beyond the window are now holding umbrellas, walking with their eyes fixed on the ground. They carry bags from pharmacies, wear Vans with no socks, sweatshirts, T shirts, hoodies.

Two girls arrive and take the table next to you. They wear drainpipe jeans and cotton hooded coats. They go off to order.

Four young men walk past the window, one of them holding his backpack above his head to shield himself from the rain. Just for a moment, he reminds you of a Roman legionary in what Plutarch called a 'tortoise formation.'

A woman with a chic bob haircut sits alone at a four-seat table across from you, looking at her reflection in her phone.

The intersection outside the window now seems like the quietest intersection in Gangnam.

The two men in the corner leave and a couple takes their places, no, two couples: older than the previous men, in collared shirts, and almost embarrassingly buxom younger women dressed to the nines. One of the women, her breasts threatening to explode the buttons off her tightly fastened cardigan at any moment—Ping! Pingping! Ping!—adjusts her bangs.

You turn your gaze to the corner behind you. The girl who once had a hair roller perched on top of her head no longer has it in her hair; instead, she now presents to the world a fetching, newly curled set of bangs.

You glance at the two smart women in sweaters and jeans at the next table. Though their bangs are already perfect, they nevertheless start to adjust them.

As you write these words, they take a selfie of themselves. Each girl primps her bangs to make sure they look just right. It's odd. One of the women extracts a tiny piece of baby clothing from a shopping bag and looks at it, holding it up with green shiny painted nails. These two women must be a couple of elegant young mothers out shopping for their kids, though the kids must have babysitters, because it's Friday night, and here they are!

Outside the window, light rain continues to fall.

A black-and-white two-tone Cube car, with extra-large wheels and tinted windows, rounds the curve of the road and disappears to your left. A black Hyundai with dark windows negotiates the corner next. There are no crowds on the street, only occasional couples.

The holiday mood reminds you that today is Thanksgiving.

The well-built girl in the too-tight sweater adjusts her bangs, runs a hand through her waist-length hair, and explains something to the man in the striped shirt sitting beside her. The rest of their party has disappeared. The three girls in the back corner are laughing and giggling rambunctiously.

No one pays the slightest bit of attention to you: you are the invisible man. And you like it that way. You are perfectly content in your unassailable corner spot.

Outside, a woman in sandals is using a sheet of paper to protect her hair from the rain. Two girls in sweatshirts are standing under an umbrella. A street cleaner in a fluorescent orange uniform is pulling a loaded garbage cart. A few more couples are stepping gingerly beneath umbrellas.

The woman with the chic bob haircut is tapping her phone with bright manicured nails and sipping her iced tea through a green straw. She runs her fingers through her bangs. In Seoul, you realize, women are obsessed with their bangs. They are forever fiddling with them. Of the ten women here, only one doesn't have bangs. Another woman slips into the coffee shop. She has a middle parting and joins Miss Chic Bob Hair. Perhaps they are nonconformists and have renounced the tyranny of bangs. But now—incredible to relate!—the embarrassingly buxom girl has just affixed a curler to her bangs and rolled it up on top of her head, where it now sits like a phylactery. She is dressed in thousands of dollars of clothes, but there she is, over there, with a hair curler on top of her head, redoing her bangs!

Nothing else moves on the street. No vehicle is passing or threatens to pass. No more tinted windows. Instead, two well made-up women stride round the corner. They are both wearing black dresses. One wears black leather ankle boots (these are very much in fashion here), the other wears high-tops with her black dress, black blouse, and a smart black coat: a vision of elegance.

A taxi turns the corner. It too has tinted windows: It's a Gangnam cab!

A woman driving a white Hyundai; her passengers are two children. They glide past the window. This is the first passing car in an hour that did not have tinted windows. A woman and a girl under an umbrella. They wear surgical face masks. They have rather frumpy outfits—wait a sec—they both have sparkling patches of silver glitter on the knees of their dungarees!

The buxom girl in the corner is still wearing her hair curler. She looks like a cross between Coronation Street's Hilda Ogden and Snow White. As you watch, she removes the curler. She brushes those bangs down. It's a sort of quick fix: stick this thing in, sit around looking funny for a bit, roll it out, and: Ta-daa—perfect bangs!

The two good-looking mothers next to you are intensely examining one of their phones, scrolling through pictures of women modelling various cosmetics. They lean together closely to scrutinize the images. The woman at the back corner, who once wore the hair curler on her head, struts forth on shiny platform shoes and totters upstairs to the washroom.

Two girls in large floppy hats stand at the counter trying to decide which cakes to get.

Across the street, a couple is kissing at the feet of the faceless sculpture. Two pairs of women and girls drift past you. The rain starts to come down heavily. A man in a black mask skitters across the intersection with odd jerky steps. A grey BMW 5-series (with tinted windows, of course) eases around the intersection curves.

A beggar slips discreetly into the coffee shop. He holds a small cardboard box and approaches each table with a bow, politely requesting money. He does not look decrepit. Perhaps because you seem to be working on your machine, he doesn't approach your table.

The three women at the corner table finally leave. You are now the one who has been on this floor the longest.

Seven animated conversations merge into a cool symphony of Hangul intonations. The sound and harmony are amazing: three cheers for Saussurean serendipity!

The elegant moms at the table next to you are doing their makeup. The one facing you (the most beautiful woman in the coffee shop) is patting her face, with — what is it called? — a mascara puff thing. She then carefully applies a sort of paste beneath her eyes. She takes out her lipstick and redoes her lips in her compact mirror. Then, she pulls another kind of mirror from her purse, opens it, inspects her bangs, and touches up her temples. God knows she doesn't need the extra grooming. Their toilette complete, they leave.

The rain is still coming down.

Six young guys in jeans and sweatshirts are hanging out by the entrance to a fried chicken place across the street. Perhaps for the dozenth time, a girl walks past, hair up in a bun, wearing what appears to be a sweatshirt and nothing else, her long bare legs ending in pumps. Presumably, some women wear short shorts under their sweatshirts, but their style requires the sweatshirt to be worn long over shorts so short that it looks like there are no shorts. They look like they are walking down the street in a sweatshirt and panties, but there must be some hidden shorts.

A silver Hyundai with tinted windows appears. A man with a multicolored golf umbrella walks by.

You have been writing for one hundred and sixteen minutes. Your temporal parameter of two hours will soon expire.

A couple of locals enters the coffee shop. The man is dressed in a white hoodless sweatshirt, baggy black pants, and white pumps. The woman is wrapped in a stunning ankle-length white cotton coat; her hair is falling luxuriously over her shoulders, cascading down her back. She wears a purple mini-dress under the long white coat and (her pièce de résistance) a pair of ankle boots with six-inch stiletto heels. The couple place their order at the counter and take their seats upstairs, the woman tottering up the stairs in her spike heels.

Across the street, a mother twirls her young daughter around by her hands.

You look over to your right to see what Miss Chic Bob Hair is up to, and, as you turn, you can't quite compute it for a minute, but there she is—transformed! Yes, she has a curler in her hair up on the top of her forehead as she sits there chatting with a friend.

The buxom girl in the about-to-burst tightly buttoned cardigan (who could certainly play Snow White in any film), the girl who so recently put a curler in her hair and sat there like a curler-crowned Ice Princess, has now taken a curler from her purse and rolled it into her hair again. The curler sits on her head like a Hasid's prayer box.

Outside, three girls in hoodies and jeans, ankles exposed (pumps with no socks) coast past with umbrellas, eating ice creams, one green, one white, one brown.

Inside the cafe, exactly forty percent of the women now have curlers in their hair.

Finally, as your allocated time here comes to an end, two slick young guys (tall and strong-looking, like Korean professional baseball players) amble around the corner holding huge umbrellas. They stride confidently along in sizeable sneakers, jeans, and sweatshirts. One of them has a plain green sweatshirt on. The other wears a white sweatshirt that has one black word printed across its chest in block capitals. As the two men approach you, the black word on the white sweatshirt gets larger with each step he takes. Like an urgent categorical imperative, more emphatic with each jump cut, the sweatshirt proclaims its incrementally insistent admonition:

THEORIZE

THEORIZE

THEORIZE

JAMES B. NICOLA

The Gentle Revolution

How it happened and exactly when, I did not notice at the time. But a gentle revolution has slowly and gradually changed the world.

My world, at any rate.

And probably yours.

* * *

The other day I saw a sign at my local library branch in Manhattan which said "Benvenidos y Benvenidas." Forty or fifty years ago, this would have been marked incorrect by Spanish teachers from any Spanish-speaking country. (If you have ever taken a Spanish class, you will know that usage varies considerably from Argentina to Mexico to Spain and everywhere in between.) Maybe even twenty years ago. Because in Romance languages (i.e., based on ancient Latin), the "masculine plural" pronoun is also the pronoun for "mixed gender plural." So it would be translated as "Welcome to all, and welcome to the ladies." But of course *ladies* are included in *all*, so that sentence is, at best, redundant and therefore bad style; at worst, it is bad Spanish.

Or was. For whoever made that statement or that sign may have simply decided that enough was enough. Men needed a suffix of their own. And that the time had come for the Spanish language—or contemporary usage—to change.

* * *

I grew up overhearing plenty of Italian and French (which are also

---

** James B. Nicola is the author of eight collections of poetry. His nonfiction book Playing the Audience: The Practical Actor's Guide to Live Performance was published in 2002 and received an award from Choice magazine.*

Romance languages) when I was a little kid, as my mom was a French teacher who spent six formative years in Italy, while my dad grew up in Quebec. My first encounter with a Romance language in *written* form, though, was the Christmas when I was in the first grade. I received (as stocking stuffers, if I remember right) two French coloring books with one word per page, plus a line illustration of a corresponding thing, hungry for the application of Crayola crayons. So I learned a slew of nouns, and also that in French it took two words to say *dog* or *table*—*le chien* and *la table*. The world of things and thoughts divided them into masculine and feminine, and you had to learn which gender went with the thing when you learned each new noun. It was a different world of words, though I suspected the world itself was pretty much the same in my home town as it was in France. Or Quebec.

Still, I looked forward to the fourth grade when, at my school, they started giving French lessons a few times a week. The year I got to fourth grade, however, they decided to have us wait till sixth grade to have French in school. That very first day of fourth grade, I must have been in a pet about it when I got home, because my mom sat me down and showed me the conjugation of two French verbs, *être* (to be) and *avoir* (to have) through two charts, two columns each, singular pronouns on the left, plural on the right: *je suis / tu es / il est / elle est // nous sommes* and so on. My mom's explanation to my inquiring mind of why the verb changed all the time was simple: Look at English, where I *am* but you *are* while he or she or it *is*. *Am*, *are*, and *is* all mean the same thing, but they are—and here was the first new word for the day—*conjugated*. And it's like that with French verbs, too, my mom said. Easy peasy.

I also learned the word *infinitive* at that session, and that in English we needed two words to make the infinitive form of the verb (*to be,* as opposed to simply *be)* while in French you only needed one. (Which made up for the higher demands of two-worded nouns, I guessed.) I learned, too, what *first person*, *second person*, and *third person* meant when it came to pronouns in French, long before the concept came up in English classes. And that French didn't have a separate word for *it*. *Il* or *elle* meant *it*, depending on the gender of the noun it stood for, its *antecedent* (another new word). Aha, I figured, a method to the madness of having to memorize the gender of each new noun.

I also learned the odd twist when it came to the plural pronouns: that *ils* and *elles* both meant *they,* whether referring to people or things, but that if the people or things were of mixed genders, *ils* covered both. *Elles* meant that all the things (or people) referred to were of the feminine gender, none of them masculine. I asked my mom, "What if you had a group of twenty girls and one boy?" *Ils.* When it came to choosing the pronoun, the one male child, or one masculine noun, canceled out all the female children or feminine nouns. "What if the ratio were a hundred or, no, a *million* feminine nouns to one masculine?" *Ils.* For a second it seemed like that wasn't fair, particularly when it involved people as opposed to mere things, but I supposed French speakers were so used to it that they never questioned it. After all, I was only *learning* French, I wasn't thinking of *changing* it.

Later that evening I recall reasoning to myself, "Well, I can only guess that assigning girls and women a plural pronoun all their own is supposed to make them more special." *Elles,* that is, made it easier to *exclude* men or males or masculine things; *ils,* on the other hand, did *not* have the "power" to exclude women, girls, females, or feminine things. The notion of cultural oppression—suggesting that an entire class of people were to be thought of as second-class citizens—didn't cross my mind; it was too horrible. Or, if it did cross my mind, I crossed it out. I was still only eight, so that wasn't too hard to do.

* * *

Later I studied Spanish and Italian, which had twice as many ways to say *you* as in French *(tu* or *vous),* four times as many as in (modern) English. In addition to regular second person pronouns, there were third-person "formal" (very polite) pronouns for *you: usted* and *ustedes* in Spanish, *Lei* and *Loro* (capitalized) in Italian. To help me get my head around this paradox, I eventually thought (again) of a parallel in English, where we might have to use a third person form when talking to a king, queen, or high-falutin' boss: "How is Madam today?" The meaning is *you,* but it is a third person form, not second, as far as conjugating that verb is concerned: "How *is,"* not "How *are."*

Along the same lines, have you noticed how versatile our pronoun *we* has become? It moonlights at times in at least a couple of ways. (1) As if its meaning were singular instead of plural. For instance: "We are not amused" signifying "*I* am not amused" (known as "the royal We"). (2) As if its meaning were *you:* such as when a waiter asks, "What are we having today?"—even when she is not eating with us.

So, as far as conjugating the verb is concerned, pronouns in English, too, can carry meanings that imply something different in person and number from what they actually are. That's language. That's usage. That's our crazy world.

* * *

There were a few other odd things I began to notice in standard American English usage or style. Once I started to learn how to read, I would pick up the mail from the mailbox and look at the addresses on envelopes, especially cards and letters from cousins, aunts, and grandparents. One day I asked an adult "Why is there *Mrs.* and *Miss* for addressing females, but only *Mr.* for guys?" That adult told me about the honorific *Master* for young men or boys. I saw this on an envelope the first time when my brother received a letter from his godparents, who had recently visited us and then returned to their home on the Canary Islands. Of course we were all over the fancy foreign stamp and postmark and whatnot, so it is no wonder I particularly noticed the whatnot, that is, the "Master George..." on the address. And for several years thereafter, even I started receiving mail from the occasional grandfather or aunt addressing me, too, as "Master James."

Recently my brother George told me that this was not quite a masculine equivalent of *Miss; Master* was only supposed to be used till a certain age, apparently, not till marriage status changed. Still, it provided a bit of parity to appease my nascent sense of, well, whatever it was I was in the nascency of sensing.

Fast forward a few years to the first issue of *Ms. Magazine* in 1970. I was a big comic book buff, and still remember seeing it with Wonder Woman on the front cover when I went to the local drug store to check out the latest comic books. I also vaguely remember reading the opening Welcome essay, right there in the drug store (was it by Gloria Steinem or Robin Morgan or both?) explaining that *Ms.* was not a new word but, rather, dated back to Elizabethan England!

Someone else in the world, I figured, had the same reaction that I had

had to the imbalance in honorifics for men and women, and thought that perhaps *Ms.* might help rectify that unfairness if it caught on in usage. I wasn't crazy, and I wasn't alone.

Although it took a few decades, *Ms.* did catch on as an honorific. I remember not so long ago when *The New York Times* announced its new editorial policy of using *Ms.* as the all-purpose honorific for women, regardless of their married status; no more Mrs. or Miss unless the lady in question specifically requested it (Mrs. Thatcher, for example). *L'Académie Française,* more recently, did something similar, with *Mme (Madame)* now replacing the former *Mlle (Mademoiselle)* when a woman was unmarried (which was nobody's business, after all, unless you wanted to ask her out for a date, right?). The times, they were a-changing, as were grammar and usage—on both sides of the Atlantic.

* * *

Here's another anomaly: In my school days, the pronoun *he* and the word *man* could refer not only to a (single) male person, but also to a single person that was male or female—that is, when the (singular) antecedent was indefinite in gender. So we were taught in English class that it was correct to say "Everyone is entitled to pursue his own dream" and "A doctor tries to prescribe appropriate medicine for his patients." The "everyone" and the "doctor" could be female as well as male, yet were to be referred to, later, by the pronoun *his*—not *her,* which, back in the day, was considered (shudder) incorrect. Likewise, *mankind* really meant *humankind* or *woman-and-mankind*, or whatnot, while "all men are created equal" in the Declaration of Independence meant "all *people* are created equal."

Or did it?

* * *

Here's another thing I noticed and wondered about. At wedding ceremonies, live, or in movies or TV shows, why did the priest or minister (or whoever) pronounce the couple "man and wife?" Why not "man and woman" or "husband and wife"—or "wife and husband" or "woman and man," for that matter?

It was somehow connected, it seemed to me, with the construction of "Mrs. Husband'sfirstname Husband'slastname" for women (e.g., "Mrs.

Reginald Smith"), the equivalent of which did not exist for men. It was years later I found out—from an episode of *All in the Family,* no less, which also premiered in 1970—that from Old Testament times till well into the twentieth century, in law as well as mindset, a wife was considered, often, to be like *property*—if not *actually* property. In many states, even into the 1970s, a woman could not get a credit card or open a checking account without a husband's name attached! Or father's, I suppose—but I really don't want to go and look this up for you, as it will make me too sad even to think about it again, once this paragraph is over. Back in 1970 I would have been eleven or twelve, and it was something so unfair, I couldn't believe it. Yet it was so.

Today, the construction "Mrs. Reginald Smith" seems antiquated, doesn't it? It has made addressing Christmas cards something of a challenge for the last few decades. And thinking about this every now and then (like when we address letters to married couples) has reminded us all, perhaps, about other gender-specific characteristics of standard American English. Consequently, we are not so averse to using *they* in place of an antiquated, *supposedly* gender-inclusive *he* (the ulterior motive of which may have actually been to be *exclusive,* not inclusive, all along).

Anyway, the same year *Ms. Magazine* and *All in the Family* debuted, so did the *Mary Tyler Moore Show.* Even a pre-teen's consciousness, like mine, couldn't help but be raised a smidgen. In the 1960s, many episodes of both *Gidget* and *That Girl* involved the heroine's trials and tribulations with boyfriends. Mary Richards, however, was an executive at WJM-TV in Minneapolis, so the story line rarely had a thing to do with her going on a date. Nor was she particularly looking for a husband. Here was something new indeed. How could anyone possibly call her "Miss Mary Richards" without also throwing her marital status into consideration and tacitly implying that it was an issue whether she was married or not—when it wasn't an issue for any male in a similar executive position? I still recall the episode, half a century ago, when she tries to convince her boss Lou Grant that she deserves equal pay even though she is a woman, and what his argument is that counters hers, and her counter to him.

* * *

A few years later, at my first college, friends told me to buy a paperback anthology of feminist essays called *Sisterhood is Powerful.* It was not a textbook for any course I took, but in those days we learned as much from fellow students as from anyone, and we often went to bookstores together. Junior year I transferred from the most socially-conscious college in the country (Clark University in Worcester, Massachusetts) to the most academically challenging (Yale in New Haven, Connecticut). My new next-door neighbor went to New York City for a season to do an internship with Robin Morgan, one of the founders of *Ms. Magazine* and, coincidentally, one of the anthologists and editors of *Sisterhood.* For some reason, this compelled me to read all the essays in that book.

Just thinking about all those novel points of view while I was still only nineteen affected me in a strange, new way; radical, yet gentle too, as if all I was doing was opening my eyes—more accurately, having them opened—and seeing what was there for the first time. I also began to look at what was possible in new ways. For instance, when someone later suggested that the word *woman* might be spelled with a *y (womyn)* so as not to be simply a derivative of *man* or *men*—well, I thought about it, and concluded that it wasn't ridiculous but made a bit of sense. A lot of sense, actually. After all, we start out physically as female embryos in the womb until about the eighth week, when males (whose chromosomes are XY as opposed to females' XX) begin differentiating in order to be born baby boys. (We now know there are other possibilities, too, so I'm not ignoring anyone who happens to be XXY or XYY, but I'll get to that later.) Of course, the use of *womyn* has not caught on, as you know. But it would not make me feel any less of a man if it did.

* * *

Anyway, in the last decades of the twentieth century, mine was not the only consciousness being raised about the intrinsic fairness or unfairness of language. For instance, when it came to pronoun choice when referring to a single person of indefinite gender (like *everyone* or *doctor),* I started to notice three new variations: (1) The complex construction *his or her,* occasionally alternating with *her or his*: "Everyone is entitled to pursue his or her own dream." (2) Alternating *he* (and *his)* with *she* (and *her)*, usually with each new paragraph. This, by the way, is the style used in my own nonfiction book.

(3) The use of *they*, a plural pronoun, even when its antecedent is singular. And here is the revolutionary evolution: A pronoun, for the first time in standard American English, would no longer need to agree in number with the noun it stood for when the gender was indefinite and if the meaning was still clear (or even clearer): "Everyone is entitled to pursue their own dream."

I was surprised to learn that as early as the mid-1980s, in a book called *The Elements of Editing,* this was officially accepted as an alternative to the old standard English version of "*his* own dream." You may be surprised to learn that this usage of *they* can be found way back in Elizabethan English!

Today you will rarely see *he* referring to an indefinite singular antecedent; you will almost always see *they,* as in *their own dream,* above. The use of *he* (to mean *everyone)* is most definitely no longer the *preferred* style, and perhaps it is not even considered the *proper* style anymore.

* * *

There has been a slow but unmistakably sure and definite change that I have witnessed in western civilization. I like to call it a Gentle Revolution. It may seem to be merely in grammar, usage, or style, but I suggest it also reflects an evolving mindset, so it gives me hope for what a culture can do to address an injustice or unfairness that seems to be merely perception or habit. And along the way, nobody was fired or jailed or killed. Probably not even yelled at.

Perhaps one day a sign in my local library will say *Benvenidas y Benvenidos y Benvenidxs,* and be translatable as "Welcome Ladies, Gentlemen, and Everyone else," to include folks who happen to be trans or simply prefer not to be included in the *-as* or *-os* suffixes in Spanish. And perhaps one day a new suffix will make a new word like *Benvenidus* or *Benvenidis* (or something else that does not exist yet) to simply mean "Welcome All," putting no particular group first but, with an enhanced sense of basic decency and mutual respect, placing all on an equal footing in our relationship to the world, to each other, and to our common humanity.

Meanwhile, in American English, all the other ways of speaking that subtly (even if unintentionally) disrespect people might slowly disappear, through the simple practice of expressing ourselves while also taking into account (even if subconsciously) what is fair and just. Eventually, we may evolve alternative ways to say things that are better: kinder, more colorful, more interesting—possibly even more *exciting*.

I realize that the kindness itself—*active* kindness—is far more important than, what should we call it, linguistic reform. But this small revolution that I have witnessed, this Gentle Revolution, has been a good one, to my way of thinking. Perhaps even a glorious one. Because it makes me just a little bit proud of the human race, and of American culture, ever-morphing, with the hope that at our core may actually lie an innate and imperturbable sense of decency and fairness.

And I know that to keep evolving in such a Gentle Revolution, to believe that we can do this sort of thing again (with our language, with our lives, and with our culture) might be just a ridiculous, childish dream of mine. But everyone should be entitled to pursue their dream. Shouldn't we?

ANN PERRINS

Asparagus, a Gift for Audrey

"There is no happiness like that of being loved by your fellow creatures, and feeling that your presence is an addition to their comfort."
—Charlotte Brontë, Jane Eyre

Living across the street from Mrs. Donn's flower and veg shop in Bearsted gave me first pick at deliveries each week. One morning before leaving for work, I was sitting in our front lounge having my morning coffee while gazing out at her shop and the Village Green. A big white van pulled up; a tall, blonde man jumped out, slid the side panel door open, and picked up several thick bundles of flowers. He carried them into the shop, then returned and grabbed a large flat of green veg that sure looked fresh. The bright tulips, orange, yellow and purple, were probably from Holland—maybe he was too. It was only about a five-hour drive from there to our little village in southeast England. I finished my coffee and strolled across the street.

As I entered the shop a little bell above the door rang, and the cool scent of fresh flowers and minty eucalyptus greeted me.

"Hello, Mrs. Donn." She was a large woman and lumbered around the crowded area behind the till. The old hardwood floor creaked as she looked up. Her soft face peeked through a mop of messy brown curls.

"Hello dear." A lot of people called me *dear* in England; it made me feel so precious.

** Ann Perrins holds a B.A. in English Literature, later graduating from law school and working internationally. After many years living in England and Central Europe, she now resides in her hometown, Portland, Oregon with her British husband, the spirit of their chocolate lab, Sasha, and the mystical trees of the Hoyt Arboretum.*

“What kind of veg did you get today?”

She lifted the wooden flat from under the till, placed it on the worktop, and began to finger through the produce.

“Let’s see… looks like we’ve got Little Gem, some Maris Piper, lots of nice-looking carrots, even rhubarb. And, what’s this? I guess asparagus.” She raised her head again, smiling.

Bushy green carrot tops draped over the side of the box, next to several bunches of bright green asparagus, wrapped in twine. The asparagus lay on their sides with ample room for their delicate little heads.

“Could I have two bunches of asparagus, please?” I decided to buy one for us and one for Audrey, my new mother-in-law. She lived up Yeoman Lane and we often took her to the grocery store, so I thought she might be pleased to receive a personal delivery instead of going out.

“Of course.” She grabbed two large bunches and laid them on brown paper, then folded it “flip-flop.”

“There you are, dear.”

I handed Mrs. Donn a pound coin. I love pound coins; they’re worth a lot more than “change” and feel more important than bills. These heavy nuggets have a nice ring-like rim around the outside. You know you have money in your pocket when you’ve got pound coins. She gave me a couple of light, less valuable coins as change. I picked up my parcel and moved aside as the next customer squeezed around me and picked out six brown eggs from the basket in the corner.

The shop was only about 400 square feet, a square room with a bay window that displayed flowers I’d just seen the driver unload: mixed tulips, long yellow gladiolas, bright purply blue irises, and red long-stem roses—all standing tall in big white buckets.

The bell rang as I shut the door behind me. I took our asparagus back home and prepared to walk up to deliver Audrey’s parcel. Again, I crossed the narrow street, with the name that always amused me. “What’s your street address?” my friends back in America sometimes asked me.

“The Street.”

“Yes, the street, what’s the street address?”

“It’s The Street. That’s the name of the street, The Street.”

“Okay, the street is The Street; is there a number?”

"Only as part of the name."

"Your house is a number, and your street is The Street?"

"Well, both. Our house is "2 Invicta Villas."

"A villa? How swank."

"It's not really a villa, just a cottage; second cottage in a row of six white connected buildings, like American row homes." Most people think of a villa as a standalone house, large with grounds, maybe. Ours was small. Two-up and two-down, rooms, that is. Originally that's truly all they were, not even a bathroom. The outhouse was in the back garden.

I often explained that these were workers' cottages from the mid-19th Century. The original metal sign is still hanging (actually half-hanging) on the wall under the roof line. Two turquoise banners say *Invicta Villas* and between them is a white horse rearing up and prepared for battle—fearless, unconquered, *Invicta.*

"Our little cottage is practically heraldic," I'd tell my friends.

I was living in our cottage with my new husband of one year, Colin, who's British. We met while working in Prague, six years before, when I was 41. I had never lived in England before. I had visited, but living there was an entirely different thing. It was like walking into the pages of my favorite English novels, classics like *Jane Eyre* for its landscape and soft manners, and stories about village life such as Barbara Pym's *Excellent Women.*

Although it was enchanting to start a new life in England, I was aware that locals don't always want foreigners around. They might meet you at the pub but won't invite you to their home.

After crossing The Street, I meandered across the Village Green, a large open grassy field, the size of a whole city block. I headed toward the large pond in the high corner of The Green. It was full of lily pads and overgrown reed beds, and was half-covered by a glorious weeping willow. A wooden bench perched just behind the pond under the old tree gave anyone sitting there a lovely, sheltered view of the village center. The British have a way of creating such picturesque, enticing natural scenes.

On this still, spring morning no one was about quite yet except for the delivery man on the lower right corner of The Green at the White

Horse pub—aptly named after that medieval horse. He was whistling a little tune as he rolled and bounced the empty aluminum beer barrel toward his truck.

We had blue sky for a change. Yes, the sun had come out! Across from the White Horse, Ron (the shopkeeper) was bringing a metal stand from his post office shop outside, to display newspapers under the awning. He waved, and I waved back. The sights and sounds of morning industry around The Green felt as much the rhythm of the day as birdsong at dawn.

I didn't know if I was walking east or west that morning. Somehow, I never knew what direction I was going in England. From The Green, you could not see hills, neither the sunrise nor the sunset; only the historic homes that framed the Green. And over my left shoulder, rose the Norman belltower of the Holy Cross Church. Every Sunday for church, every Tuesday for practice, and on special occasions, local bell ringers pulled the long ropes. The huge bell swung to and fro and the clapper struck the inside of the bell rim; the most beautiful clanging echo spread across the village.

Our church blessing was at Holy Cross Church the year before. It had been a long engagement, since Colin had had a sticky divorce, as some are. It was hard on all of us. I remember the Vicar asking if we wanted bell ringers at the ceremony. I said "Sure," thinking we'd have several people standing, taking turns ringing little handbells. Was I surprised when we walked outside after the ceremony, to hear the loud ding-dong announcement to the world that we were, in fact, married. Those bells rang for fifteen minutes as we stood in the old churchyard with our guests, unable to hear each other speak. It was a great preface to living in the village—maybe to married life as well.

Still on the mission to deliver my asparagus, I walked further past The Green and did not stop to rest upon the inviting bench near the pond. Continuing up Yeoman Lane, I passed more old houses: Snowfield, an imposing estate mostly hidden by a tall yew hedge, and the diminutive Coach House that guarded it a long time ago.

Turning right on Tower Lane, I passed the old vicarage, a Tudor home with black timber frames and an old beautiful wooden front door with a brass lion head knocker. Audrey's home was down the next street. She and her husband Brian bought it in the 50's, newly built on carved-up nursery land. It was a traditional three-bed semi-detached red brick dwelling; the front door was inside a recessed porch covered with a rounded archway. A spacious garden in the back of the house had originally been planted out with vegetables and fruit trees: apple, pear, and greengage plums, producing enough to feed their family of four for the winter. Later, it was landscaped with a lawn and shrubs, and a shed plus a garage was added. The house was solid and secure, just like Audrey.

As I walked up to the house that day, I thought to myself how comforting it was to have a mother-in-law of my own, who was also so kind to me. We had nothing at all in common, except of course, her son. But from the very beginning, she accepted me—a foreigner—wholeheartedly. When you have a nice mother-in-law, it's like an unexpected Christmas gift.

The first time Colin brought me to England to meet his parents was over Christmas. I was pretty nervous, overwhelmed by the regular stage fright one has when meeting potential in-laws, especially as a foreigner. And besides, there was the uncomfortable fact that he was not yet divorced.

We'd met at a running club at Prague's *Holeŝovice* train station. It felt like we had known each other for a hundred years. That, plus his clear blue eyes and gentle manner made it hard to walk away. I guess we were both a little lonely, too. Working in a foreign country can be like that, especially when you're not fluent in the language. We agreed to visit together some of the exquisite classical concerts in town, the Prague Guitar Quartet, the Czech Philharmonic, that sort of thing, and have a bite to eat afterwards. Prague had endless enticing and intimate venues to explore. Of course, one thing led to another.

When I met his parents that first Christmas, Colin was in the middle of his divorce, and I assumed his parents were not happy about it. I thought they were probably attached to his ex-wife, the mother of their grandchildren, and would deeply resent me. But Audrey and Brian welcomed me with open arms, full of hospitality and smiles.

"Good morning! We're so pleased to finally meet you! Welcome to Bearsted!" Brian said, opening the front door, touching my shoulder, and kissing me on the cheek. Audrey stood next to him wearing a blue gingham pinny to protect her dress (as she did most days, always in the middle of cooking something).

"Yes, come on in, please! Come to warm up!" she chimed, moving aside. That morning was a "hoar" frost. The landscape—the branches of the trees and shrubs, even the telephone wires—was covered with a very fine layer of soft ice. Locals said it looked like "the white feathers of frost on an old man's beard." Everything glistened in silence and took my breath away.

We all sat in the lounge with the gas fire on and got acquainted before lunch. They did not appear disturbed by the divorce, at least not about my part in it. Before long, I realized they were not close to their former daughter-in-law, and that there were good reasons why the marriage fell apart that had nothing to do with me.

On that cold winter day, Audrey served smoked haddock with mashed potatoes, poached eggs, and peas. (One always has peas with fish in England.) The haddock was slightly smoked with a yellow-orange tinge on the outside but soft, white delicate fish inside. The poached eggs were made the old-fashioned way, boiled in a pot of water with a little vinegar, so they were imperfectly shaped and slightly runny. That meal is one of my favorites to this day.

"Won't you have more to eat?" Brian constantly tried to get me to have seconds and thirds, but eventually I convinced him that I just couldn't manage another bite. He had a soft, swirly accent, and was always smiling and solicitous. I came to learn that his grey cardigan, a dress shirt and tie, and smart shoes was his usual outfit.

It gave me a warm feeling to remember that first meeting with them as I walked up to the house with my asparagus. I rang the bell and saw the curtains move aside as Audry checked to see who was at the door. She greeted me in her usual polite, cheerful way:

"Hello dear, how nice to see you," she said smiling wide. I told her about the fresh asparagus from Mrs. Donn and proudly showed her my parcel.

"Oh, thank you. That's so kind of you," she said, but glanced skeptically at the parcel. "Won't you come in for a cup of tea?" She opened the door wider.

Audrey was neither short nor tall, a good height for a woman in her late seventies, about a foot shorter than me but I'm pretty tall, and she had strong legs. Her wavy brown-grey hair framed a broad forehead. I always admired her large, very round azure eyes, the color of the sky on a clear day. That morning, she was still in her sleepwear: a long nightgown, and floral wraparound dressing gown with waist tie, plus lavender dearfoam slippers.

"Sure, Audrey, I'd love to." I followed her into the house. We walked down the narrow-carpeted hallway past the stairs and into the tiny kitchen where, with the flick of a switch, she turned the electric kettle on. People in England often ask, "Put the kettle on, won't you?" when they're in need of a cup of tea, as though it's the biggest chore in the world. Audrey actually flicked two switches: one at the wall outlet, one on the kettle. She always double-did everything security-wise; turn the lamp off at the bulb, then turn it off at the outlet. Lock the door, check it, then re-lock it again.

As it was morning, Audrey's transistor radio was playing, perched on the kitchen window ledge. The window looked out through the conservatory to the garden, with a picturesque wooden bench underneath an apple tree. English wooden benches always look alive sitting in a garden so comfortably, happy to have a sheltered place just to be.

Because it was Monday, the laundry was in a basket ready for the outside line. Laundry is always done on a Monday in England, baking on Thursday, fish for dinner on Friday, roast dinner on Sunday. This makes deciding what to cook for dinner a lot easier.

The radio was playing BBC Radio One, a station hosted that day by a youngish male DJ who had a distinctive, pleasant (but not too cheerful), informative voice, and a quietly refined, not overdone English accent.

The kettle began to boil and switched itself off. She placed triangular PG Tips tea bags in two narrow mugs for steeping.

"Sugar today, dear?"

"No, not today, thanks." She added "just a half" to her own, as usual.

The mugs were porcelain, for the British know the best tea ware is porcelain or bone china, because they're both non-porous. Tea mugs and cups have wide rims so they can be sipped, not gulped—for a good cup of tea must be *hot*. There was something so pleasant about having an old-fashioned cup of tea, in old-fashioned tea mugs, served by an old-fashioned mother-in-law, in her warm home. I could put my hectic working world behind me and focus on nothing more than "having a natter." The English are so genuine when having a simple, friendly conversation about nothing.

Audrey turned the radio off, and I heard the soothing song of collared doves from her garden: koo-KOO-kook, koo-KOO-kook.

"How's mother?" she asked me, as she often did.

"She's fine. I spoke to her yesterday and they've had a lot of rain in Oregon this spring."

Audrey's house was not overly formal, and neither was she. She grew up as a farmer's daughter, a no-nonsense woman. In her teens, her father bought a fish-and-chips shop on Ashford Road in Bearsted, and she worked there too, frying up cod, hake, haddock, and chips in big baskets of hot peanut oil. She was working there when Hitler bombed that part of Kent with his V-2 rocket-propelled bombs. She survived by diving under tables, managing to avoid the hot splashing oil. But that day the building cracked in two.

As a widow she kept to herself, content to see her family and neighbors and talk on the phone once a week to her childhood friend, also named Audrey. Although they lived only ten miles away from each other, they didn't feel the need to visit in person, just to talk on the phone for an hour or so every Friday. When my mother-in-law finally passed away at eighty-nine (some ten years after my visit that morning), the other Audrey died a week later.

"Slice of toast, dear?"

"That sounds nice, sure."

"Marmalade? Or maybe marmite this morning?"

"Oh marmalade, please." I had not yet acquired a taste for marmite. That savory spread was a bit too yeasty for me, especially first thing in the morning. But British marmalade—what a treat. It's the perfect mix of bitter and sweet, with tangy little peels of Seville oranges swimming on top of buttery toast. A great way to brighten so many grey English mornings.

Audrey did not use a pot of tea as they often do on TV because that's only for special occasions. She toasted the bread, always square Hovis white bread, buttered generously edge to edge, and sliced down the middle.

While the tea was steeping, I laid the parcel on her worktop and opened the crinkly paper. My grassy asparagus with slightly purplish heads lay there like babies waiting to be changed.

"Here they are, can't get any fresher than this," I offered.

"Lovely dear. I'll get a vase."

"Oh, Audrey. No, no, they're not flowers they're vegetables, for eating!"

"Really? Well, I never. I've never seen such a thing. But I don't really need more veg; I've got plenty for now. You and Colin keep them."

I hadn't considered that Audrey, being ever the local farmer's daughter, wasn't privy to non-native asparagus. She had her select menu of traditional British cooking and did not waver from it. Asparagus is not native to Britain; it came from the east Mediterranean. I always loved it, a spring delicacy.

"But I already bought us a bunch; these are for you! Do you know how to cook them?"

"I don't suppose I do. I could boil them." Audrey usually boiled her veg to a pulp, so I cautioned her.

"Don't boil long, steaming is best. Place them in shallow water, *after* it's already simmering, for about three minutes."

"They don't look like they'd fit in the saucepan, shall I cut the tops off?"

"No! No! That's the best part, just break off the bottom like this." I grabbed one stalk and bent it with both hands; the tough yellowy bottom part snapped off with a crack.

"That looks easy." She snapped the bottom of another stalk and laughed.

The tea was ready by then, so she removed the soggy teabags, added a little milk, placed the mugs and toast on a plastic tray, and picked it up.

"Come on into the lounge, dear; we'll have our tea."

I followed her down the hall and into the lounge, where she set the tray on a big ottoman and we sat down in comfy, overstuffed chairs. The chairs next to the sofa faced a large bay window that looked out to her front garden. Hydrangeas were beginning to bud in the right corner of the garden and we had a sweeping view of the neighborhood.

Audrey and I chatted about the weather, the latest news, family events. I told her about my frustrations at work. Colin and I had our own engineering business nearby with a dozen electricians working for us. We were learning that England was a tough place to do business. Behind the façade of polite English manners, people were shrewd and cut-throat. I told her about some of our problems with employees quitting without notice, making it difficult to fulfill our contracts.

"Well, I never." She shook her head. "You shouldn't pay them!"

"They quit the day they received their paychecks direct to their bank accounts, so we didn't owe them anything. They planned it that way."

"I don't believe it. Why would they do such a thing?"

"You tell me."

"I wish I could help. Is there anything I can do? I could loan you some money," she offered.

"Oh Audrey, no—no. We'll figure it out." I couldn't believe she would so easily loan us money when she certainly wasn't rich. She didn't have a credit card, or a bank account, not even a checkbook. She lived off her husband's pension and handled all her financial transactions at the local post office or in cash—proud not to owe anyone anything.

Eventually, we talked about what we always ended up talking about: the latest shenanigans by Colin's ex. Some spouses split up, divide their assets, and go their merry (or not so merry) way. Others hang around coming up with ways to get back at their ex. She was the latter. Colin was still trying to recover a few of his possessions from their twenty-five-year marriage, since he had left home for his assignment to Prague with only two suitcases and had never been allowed to retrieve his belongings. The divorce decree allocated him a list of twenty personal items, such as his grandmother's chest, his Hofner 12-string guitar, and some family photos.

"Has she given back my mother's Victorian chest yet?"

"No. But she mailed Colin the key to a storage locker where she says his things have been sent."

"What on earth? Why doesn't she bring him his things? They're not hers; it's the least she can do after all the money she got. That's nonsense. I'll never understand that woman. Well, you two never mind all that. Go get his things from the storage locker, send back the key, and phooey to her."

Audrey reached around to the side table by her chair where she kept her personal business. The area was her private bureau. She twisted around, began fishing through things, brought out her coin purse and pulled out a £20 note. She reached over and held it toward me, extending her arm straight as she looked away.

"Here, you two go out for a nice meal after you get his things back and forget about the past. Their marriage was over a long time ago and everyone needs to move on." She waved the money up and down in front of me. "Go ahead, take it, I won't have it back."

"Audrey, you don't need to do that."

"Yes, I insist. Treat yourselves, you've both been working hard, and that divorce went on far too long. Go on, take it."

"Gosh, that's so sweet of you. If that's what you want, we'll do as you like." I took the £20 note and slipped it into my pocket. It *had* been a long divorce: from his departure for work in Prague some six years prior, our meeting, the realization his marriage was broken, the back and forth of what to do, the going back home to try to "make it work," the teenage children and their visits (or non-visits), the expensive, drawn-out legal proceedings, and on and on.

"I do feel bad the divorce cost so much, and Colin lost so many of his things," I said, looking down.

"Everyone deserves to be happy. Don't you feel bad. They were just things." She shook her head again.

"I don't know. I just don't know" she murmured. "Imagine, a storage locker and a key in the mail...nonsense!"

She bit into her last slice of toast and took another sip of tea. Soon after, I thanked her for the tea, said my goodbyes, and she thanked me for the asparagus. We stood up and walked to the doorway, where I kissed her soft cheek, and departed.

Crossing the street, I looked back and saw Audrey standing at the bay window. She always watched us go, whether we left on foot or by car. She once told me how she loved to stand at that window and watch Colin walk down the road to his primary school, wearing the little grey worsted wool shorts and navy-blue blazer, knee socks with black shoes, and a cap with his school's badge on the front. Perhaps it was like watching the sunset, where the sun becomes smaller and smaller until eventually it's out of sight.

It always made me a little sad to leave her, as it did to leave my own mother, knowing they were widows and lived alone, their busy lives behind them, while my hectic life was pulling me forward.

As I turned the last corner toward the public footpath, I waved at her and she waved back. I thought, *it's half past twelve; Audrey is probably going to cook lunch now. Since it's Monday, she'll surely be making Bubble & Squeak using Sunday's leftovers, with a cold slice of roast.*

Walking back toward Invicta Villas, I slipped through the wooden turnstile near the old churchyard. As I passed the tall worn tombstones where daffodils were popping up, I suddenly realized that Audrey would probably not be cooking or eating that asparagus. But they must have made an interesting display, in a vase on her windowsill, next to the transistor radio.

PETE WARZEL

Damage

"There are levels past which things no longer connect."
- Warren Zevon, New York Times, January 26, 2003

4:25 PM, Sunday afternoon, July 27, 2025, and all is well in Santa Fe. It is quiet, the weekend closing down, time between art markets and visitor invasion. A full month before Zozobra, the annual Santa Fe witch-burning for fifty thousand wild-eyed spectators. We are packing up to drive back to Denver after a week of working on the house and visiting with friends. It is a peaceful moment in the day, the weather performing up to afternoon summer standards, hitting 93 degrees right at about the time noted.

I take a bag of garbage to the cans behind the wall at the street. The street is Galisteo, at the intersection of Booth coming in from the east. This is a residential neighborhood, South Capitol, where people know each other and are friendly, helpful. I am midway in our gravel parking area when I see a Subaru driving down Booth to the stop sign at Galisteo. My senses are tuned to a frequency unknown to me.

The car does not stop, but crosses Galisteo to jump the curb into our street wall, twenty feet away from where I am walking. The noise makes me momentarily nauseous and I see the stucco wall come apart like a slow-motion film of buildings being detonated, concrete block beneath the stucco scattering and a large slab collapsing on the pyracantha shrub, otherwise healthy with orange berries this time of year. The bush kept pieces of wall from flying at me. I drop the garbage and move quickly to the north edge of the shattered wall to help the

** Pete Warzel has published poetry, short fiction, essays, interviews, nonfiction articles, and book reviews in national and international literary journals, as well as in regional and national magazines and newspapers. He lives in Santa Fe and Denver.*

helpless driver. He simultaneously backs up, driving in reverse backing down Booth Street, fast, weaving. He was looking at me, not dazed or startled; resolved. I hear a second crash, wood splintering and the screech of metal torquing. Now I run across Galisteo thinking this guy really needs help.

At the stop sign I hear the engine and wheels and see him coming fast down Booth again. He looks distinctly at me again, and he is not going to stop so I scuttle north thinking that this neighbor's fence has enough linear feet to stop him. What the fuck, this guy is trying to hit me. He guns across Galisteo one more time and into the drive entry of our house, through the lattice fence that surrounds the main courtyard and stops, wood posts splintering, lattice snapping, the engine winds up and I can hear wheels trying to turn, spitting gravel, in reverse. He is ready to flee the shattered fence wood and ivy and rose bush stalks that now cover the car, but he cannot. The car's wheels are jammed with detritus and the Subaru is bound by vines and thorns.

I run to the guest house and hear Denise talking on the phone. I yell for her to call 911. She comes out of the door after me as I head for the courtyard. Our neighbor, Will, from directly across Galisteo, is already at the driver's door, speaking calmly to the driver, telling him to relax and turn off the car. He is in reverse, intent to back out of the damage, *trying*, I think in retrospect, *to make it all go away*. He looks at me again through the window. Crazed eyes. Distant but focused. I hear Denise in the parking area loudly explaining the situation to the 911 operator.

There is water pouring from the outside faucets on the house wall and Will is in control so I run back into the guest house for a wrench to turn off the water. When I return to the courtyard another neighbor is helping Will calm the driver. The demands coming from the driver's mouth are disheartening. Will reaches through the car window and shuts it off, the electronic key still in the driver's pocket. Quiet. Extremely quiet. It's the silence of damage.

I wait until the car is turned off to get between it and the wall and work on the water. I am not successful and the neighbors fear the liquid is gas leaking from the car.

I hear Denise on the phone again giving directions, quick description of what she sees, "Is he injured?" asking for ambulance and police. "Get away from the car Pete, now," she yells at me. I go back to the wall and the water, stepping on wood slats, wire, the tangle of ivy and the thorns of what were three eight foot tall rose bushes. Clay sherds from pots crunch as I make way, electrical wire from the patio lights and a mess of torn up irrigation tubing, glass. The car door opens and the neighbors have the driver out. He is stumbling in the tangle. He looks at me again while they hold him and only later that evening I think that he has looked at me four times, directly, making eye contact with those eyes that were really not right, but focused, clearly focused on me.

The two neighbors help him walk through the entry hole in the fence, a good fifteen feet of now empty space, and he keeps trying to go out into the street. "I want to go home." He is not shouting but delivers the message in a monotone, a voice controlled, deliberate, entitled. "I am going home. Call Richard." He sounds like a little boy. He is a large man and he sounds like a boy pouting and muttering in defiance, and not backing away from what he wants. "Richard is on his way," says an unseen neighbor. "I want to go home," and the emphasis is on "I want."

Someone takes a chair from the dining table in the courtyard and brings it out to the sidewalk. The neighbors get him to sit. I am back at the water but it keeps pouring out, irrigating the now uprooted green of the courtyard that no longer needs sustenance. I give it up.

Richard appears. He is willing to get his husband on his feet and walk him down Booth Street to their home. Neighbors are everywhere, surrounding the seated driver, on the corners of Booth, on the sidewalks on Galisteo. It is a confused street carnival. Michael, the driver, stands up and lurches to walk, but Denise tells Richard that "He can't leave. No! If he leaves the scene he will be in worse fucking trouble than he is now," and so Richard pushes Michael back into the chair and shouts "Michael, sit." Richard is not happy, his bald head sweating, but he is not panicked. Michael is even less happy, jaw clenched, sulking really. Denise has done him a favor.

Cars are coming down one way Galisteo and I move into the street to stop them, thinking that Michael is going to succeed in bolting into the street and get slammed by an impatient Santa Fe driver in a big ass pickup truck. The crowd starts yelling at me to let them through and I tell them they are fucking crazy that he will run into the street. "No, he won't. He's sitting." What, really? I saw him leave two accidents and you think he is going to sit because you want him to? The first driver is giving me an angry look.

Richard introduces himself to me and now it appears that many of the neighbors know the two of them. Medics get Michael on a gurney and into the back of an ambulance. A fire engine is there probably to hose down the gas that is really water and I go looking for the cop in charge, seeing now two SFPD vans parked on Galisteo. I see two firemen in the courtyard working on the broken faucets and they somehow turn the water off. The afternoon gets quiet again. SFPD is not controlling traffic but I think it is not my problem anymore.

The neighbor on the south east corner of Booth and Galisteo is telling someone that he hit the fence and front yard of Robin's house on Booth, then hit our wall and ran through the fence across the parking area. I tell her that "No. That is not what happened. I saw every second of it and you are passing on bad information. Let's get the story right, so the cops get it right. The cops need to get it right." She apologized to me twenty minutes later when calm returned to the South Capital neighborhood, the Don Gaspar Historic District of Santa Fe, New Mexico.

Sergeant Laramie comes to me. I explain what I saw; perhaps. I see it all, I can play the entire path of destruction in my head. "Michael is not hurt," he says. "The air bags did not inflate." He has cuts on his legs from falling in the detritus of the courtyard, and he is invisible in the ambulance. "You are a good witness."

Denise asks me, "Why did you run across the street when you saw what was going on?"

When I showed Sergeant Laramie my identification for witness purposes he did a double take. My New Mexico driver's license had the same address of the driver of the Subaru who just ran through my property, twice. I had lived in what is now their home: a four apartment courtyard home with a grand horse chestnut tree brought in from Missouri in the 1850's. My then landlord sold the place to this couple several years ago and moved to Pennsylvania where his wife died in a quick onslaught of cancer that crashed into everybody like this car registered at the same address. I had changed the address on my license digitally, but the New Mexico Department of Motor Vehicles did not update my card. The irony was despicable.

The sergeant, spooked, tells me there will be two investigations, one for the accident and a criminal one. I think, *well, there were three accidents.* Two of which he left the scene, the third he tried to leave the scene, once in a car that would not move and again by foot. How do you sort that out? How do you charge it? I ask Laramie if they have any police tape to put across the wide gap in the courtyard fence so people will not step in tomorrow to look at what happened. Tourists and locals walk down the street to downtown and they will be curious, perhaps thinking this is now public space. As most people in Santa Fe believe all space to be public for their enjoyment. The cops do not have any tape but I am promised they will get some and come back to signify the space with SFPD, *Do Not Cross.*

I cannot remember what Denise and I ate that night but I can tell you every detail of the three minutes of the three crashes. When I was in bed trying to read for a while, Denise followed, tucked me in and said "I know you keep things inside but that must have been traumatic for you." What? "Almost getting hit." No, I saw it all happen, and it was just footage in a bad documentary. She continued, "Why did you get near the car in the courtyard when he was still trying to back away? What were you thinking?" I was trying to see if I he needed help but the neighbors had him under control so I was trying to shut down the water. "But you could have been hit while he was trying to back away." No, I didn't go to the faucets until the car was turned off and I never got behind the car, the hawthorn tree was in the way.

The tow truck driver worked slowly and elegantly to draw the car back out of the wreckage without damaging my beloved hawthorn.

The next evening, Monday, our friend Ken took Denise and me to dinner at Jinja to get away and forget the scene of the crime. They each have martinis and I have a Mai Tai, just to be fantastical. While Denise is in the restroom I see Michael and Richard come in through the door into the bar and I am facing them. They do not see me and when Denise returns I put a finger to my lips and then point to my left to the two men on bar stools. "No." Ken says, "No. Holy shit."

Michael has been released that afternoon from custody, either jail or hospital, I do not know which, but here they are, perhaps celebrating also. They are not drinking alcohol. Both men look perfectly content, gleaming, put together. I whisper to Denise that we cannot just ignore them and she nods so we both rise and take three steps to the bar. The conversation is guarded, quiet, neither of them seem disturbed and that disturbs Ken, immensely. They both apologize, Richard more than Michael. Michael looks at me again, square in the eyes, and truly seems clueless about the entire situation. This is the first time he has officially met me, but he knows me. He apologizes. I have the distinct feeling that his thoughts are vacant.

They say goodbye when they finish eating and walk out steadily. Ken shakes his head, and I receive an email from him the next morning advising me to rethink our relationship with my new best friends, saying they are entitled and tone deaf, not good people.

I do rethink it all. All. The damage is more than stucco and concrete, wood and landscaping. The real damage is unseen, the worry and work of putting back together homes, ours and the neighbor's down the street whose yard was torn up, fence torn down, when new tenants were arriving in two days' time, the former guests sitting in the chairs that Michael blew apart with his back bumper less than ten minutes before he hit. Hit indiscriminately, three times, three separate incidents, three sets of damage.

The damage in full was lost on Michael and Richard. It was, anyhow, less than they could conjure. No pedestrians on a busy walking street, no parents walking their kids to the school playground, no parked cars, no oncoming cars on a heavily trafficked access route to downtown Santa Fe. A few minutes either way would have been more appalling ruin. Despite the damage, there's luck, and there's an expectation they could truly make it all go away. They had no idea of the Subaru hitting the house wall within the courtyard a foot from a new propane tank I had connected to the grill that morning, and a foot to the right where the two gas meters for the house and guest house were situated. No sense of the nonsense involved in wanting to get away a third time by backing out of the carnage of the courtyard through another section of fence into the parking area where two cars were parked, ours and our guest's. My beautiful hawthorn stopped the senselessness, more reason to love the tree, as I do.

Fall and winter are coming now and the tree will turn red with berries, stark against the snow that will be here in several months. In the spring white blossoms will burst, bringing life back to a gray world, then leaf green and host the birds that amaze me when they land in the green and avoid the thorns as long as finishing nails. What will I think of this when that spring comes, and have had time to reflect on the damage?

My neighbors gather on Tuesday night across the street in Heather's front yard, behind an undamaged fence, and take issue with me that this was something different. "He was drunk, he had no idea what he was doing." Maybe. But, I saw him look at me, aware, angry, not at me I suspect, but at something. If you hit a wall you stop and decide either to wait for the police and your fate, or run to another fate altogether. He drove away twice, deliberately. "No it can't be deliberate if you are drunk and do not know what you are doing." Right. He knew what he was doing, I, with a DUI conviction to my illustrious name, think. Muscle memory does not work out the logistics of what he attempted to do, but it also did not have the capacity to pull it off. To me it was an intentional run but I cannot articulate a sense of that other than just living the minutes as he went from one crash to another and his looking into my eyes.

Robin texts me on Tuesday and asks if we can talk. She is the owner of the house down Booth Street where Michael backed through her fence and into the front sitting area her guests had just vacated. She comes over and visits with Denise and me to vent her cycle of disbelief, first concern for Michael, then anger. She is pissed and lost as she tries to handle the steps to bring order to the chaos in her front yard, dismiss the thought of what if her guests were still sitting in the wooden chairs that now have been garbaged away as sticks and splinters, all parts of the damage.

People walk by all week and take photos of the wall, the gap in the fence, the interior of the courtyard they have never seen before. They are unknowing folks, they do not understand it all but see the physical damage.

"What did you tell them, Richard?" Michael asked in a whisper as he was forced to sit in my chair and await the police. "What did you tell them?"

I will never know what Richard did not tell anyone. Bigger damage, I presume, the damage of human beings, done to each other, intimately yet publicly.

ANN MARIE GAMBLE

Just Asking

People keep asking me
Am I upset about my dad's health?
And I tell them the real question is
whether my dad is upset about it
It is, after all, his health
He has been remarkably sanguine
Reformulating processes
pointing out that he has passed
the average lifespan
So really the question is:
Am I upset about my dad's age?
It is just math,
you might as well rage at gravity
My age makes his age
And that is the real question:
Am I upset for what's to come?
This has an inevitable conclusion

Those are his words: "inevitable conclusion"
And I know now
Knowing the story frees you up
Lets you take your eyes off the map
Look out the window
And talk
Without calculating the mileage

---

* *Ann Marie Gamble is an editor and writer. In her free time, she organizes volunteers for the Unbound Book Festival and checks out as many audiobooks as the library allows.*

Trying

If I were good at this
my stanzas engraved over doorways
you'd see how you're necessary
Not just to my world
not just threads in the fabric of my days
but the sun
You would not question the space you hold
the shadows you cast
If I could find a metaphor so true
I would need to find others,
like hypothetical pillars fanning out
from the real foundation of you
If I were a physicist
and you my theorem
about the order of the universe
with proofs and consequences
We would get an A on you
for the degree
for our certification in life
our mastery of the world
If only I could put my pen down
and tell you what I mean

Ode to the Peach

I am going to show
my appreciation
by eating you up, my fruity friend
And breath in
your perfume
floating from the windowsill as we wait while your chemistry
finishes its work
Deepening the blush across your shoulders
softening your belly
and pulling the sugars from your cells.
My teeth will burst your tight skin,
caressed by fuzz,
shivering in anticipation.

Just Write

They say if you want to know
how the writing is going, see how clean
the writer's house is.
Mopping this isn't procrastination,
it's productive.
We've got to get to the back
of these closets someday.
The dishwasher chugs through a cycle.
"Pause cleaning," the robot vacuum chirps.
"Device may be suspended in air.
Move to a new position and try again."
I try a chair on the porch.
Stare at a different neighbor's garage.
A breeze tries to riffle pages
but my pen presses back.

The Cashier

In the morning, the cash drawer is light and empty
And I spring to the side with each sale
A sashay of the hips when I hit "Total"
The drawer shoots forth to welcome the coins
In one hand, one click per digit, one beep per sum
The other shifts goods towards their new home
The line weaves back to the deli counter for lunch
The hum of the fluorescents grows more angry
Crowded by trade, the cash drawer changes tempo
Instead of a dodge, a crash
Coins flail,
Lose their momentum
Against my belly
Dribble to the floor
Exact change lost
To the dust under the counter
I'm out of dimes
And flex in one of my knees
One guy, one loaf of bread
Another has gotten the last pie
The "Closed" sign is up
The door locked, front lights dimmed
I sit while I count
Re-empty the drawer for these heavy arms to carry

An Early Morning Along the Road to the Lake

Today one of the joggers is riding a bike
I have decided the two are father and son
They look alike in the way humans do
But we are out along a row of vacation cottages
Where people introduce themselves
by how many generations
have been coming here
Probably the cousins all say,
"Skeet's the spitting image of Howard
at that age, don't you think?"
And then it's off to the time he and
Dougie forgot to tie up the canoe
Skeet has been going by Peter for decades
And Harold is actually quite proud of him
Hauls his retired bones out of bed
every morning he's here
For some time together in the cool woods
Pete for his part leaves out the sprints,
found a secondhand bike for every third day
He doesn't need to jog every single day,
but Christ, the cousins
And so this quiet time shared with Pops
A smiled good morning to the dog walker
coming the other way

COLLIN GARRITY

Leafblower

I acknowledge the stupidity of a leafblower,
spreading peas on a plate to hide them
after we planted these trees above a flat unbroken
web of concrete from here to mexico

today we are judged by how botoxed we keep
our lawns. but in musuems, remains are labeled
by the tools found with them. all we know of
this partial skeleton is that he carried a hammer.
this one was burried with a sword and belt buckle
I carry a leaf blower, judge me by something else.

with headphones on, I scatter grass clippings
lamenting the time I gave away my best pocket knife
leaving me with only one pocket knife. but
it is enough knives. what would I do with more?

** Collin Garrity lives in St Louis USA where he writes poetry and renovates brick buildings. He studied poetry at Warren Wilson College.*

Hospital Poem

This prolonging slow decay
we have chosen for ourselves
is a stupid death

white walled,
a crowded and lonely place
to leave a ghost

is it possible
this prayer is the last new thought
before an infinite climb?

is all that's left,
a stairwellian loop chore
short lived and long lasting
spent not naked
but not clothed?

Naked Polaroid Vending Machine

It's just a mirror in the woods
that you come across
when you are sleeping.
you have choices to make
a slot for dollar bills, a mouth to drop into
you surprise yourself by adding to it

slowly releasing the button on your pants
you twist to mask the rolls and then
you do not wait to see the image appear

you drop it as an offering in a donation slot,
a locked box tethered to an elm
like a dear stand waiting ready
for a hunter to pass the hours in calm autumn stillness
then either go home, or kill

Bathroom Floor

A woman sits clipping her toenails on the floor
blue sweater, no pants, curls spilling to hide her face

what I lost I lost slowly
lost all at once but in echoes
woke up each day thinking about it
lost but always knew where it was
lost not like a key but like a game

lost it long before I lost it, lost it wholly,
once I started knowing I would lose

what I lost I am still losing, no longer
at the moment of waking, I forget again
and again each day until it means nothing to forget

blue sweater, cotton swab in her ear
eyes closed in front of the mirror

Skin On

In the scalding bathtub, pink skinned, I am the soup.
sweat brined and shame spiraling about something I said
at a wedding fifteen years ago

I take no comfort knowing our names will remain
carved into softening stone long after we extinct ourselves
to prove whatever point

I soap the soft imagined bottoms of my feet,
a lemon scented unseen hand turns the water slowly cold
my eyes will not stay open. willow tree, empty lot

I drift, but I will not give up my favorite decoration.
I make a sparse broth, my legacy is a worn pair of shoes

I embody the hostile architecture of a curved bench
I accept the docile takeover of a flock of crows
I acknowledge the obvious stupidity of a leafblower

OLIVIA SOULE

The Deep End of the Pool

You were King Poseidon.
You taught me what vests
to wear when it wasn't
deep. You let me fall
into the deep end of the pool.
Now, I'm found in your
own deep. Now, I'm lost
in my own blue. Now, 10 feet
will be too deep. Now, 10 mgs
Mr. Morphine won't be enough
to give me relief.

You were King Midas.
You taught me what vests
to wear when it wasn't
blue. You let me fall
into the deep end of the pool.
Now, 10 feet will be too
deep. Now, 10 mgs Mr. Morphine
won't be enough to give me relief.
Now, I'm lost in your own
deep. Now, I'm found in my own
blue. The blue end of the pool.

---

* *Olivia Soule completed her M.F.A. in poetry at the University of Nevada, Reno in 2018. She has a B.A. in English and Italian from UCLA and has studied in Bologna, Italy. She published a poetry chapbook titled Reflections in 2025.*

computers don’t have feelings

computers don’t make apologies
don’t process repentance
they don’t have feelings
tom & sue are poor specimens
to process this they killed ‘em
to test ‘em for one less thing

computers don’t make apologies
they don’t contemplate
plate glasses of respect
don’t collate expressions of regret
scheduled to cry on Friday
their mathematical references
computers don’t have feelings

Blood Draws in Los Angeles

Today, I'm not available
to be your human pincushion.
Sitting in that hospital chair
for the nth number of times.
10 vials of blood drawn
til it makes me dizzy.
Orange juice & tears
and just like that
my heart torn open.
Blood spewing everywhere
like the Manson family murders.

These cleansing tears a catharsis,
like purging the ashes of you
and the nightmare experience
you abandoned us all with.
You are not suffering anymore,
so why am I still
suffering for you?

When my astrocytoma
was first discovered, you wept
inconsolably in the Expedition.
You called me "incorrigible".
I don't blame you- you were
coping the best way you knew,
which was not well– it was better
the way that Mom kept
the stiff upper lip.

Meanwhile, my senses were
blunted, unable to process
whether I was going to live
or die at 21 years of age.
Daddy, little did you know
you would not have to see me die.
I would have that privilege.

Ghost of you,
ghost of me,
ghost of OCD.
You joked
you would haunt me.
Since last Thursday,
I have entered
a wormhole of insanity.

In recovery, they say you
have "Cadillac Problems",
but these are not.
These are problem problems.
I don't want to suffer
for you
anymore.
I'm suffering enough for myself.
Plenty of suffering
to go around.
Tonight,
I will
sleep sound.

TY CRONKHITE

Ode to the Ellipses

They stand
like the president of a country
for something not there
or something left undone

unsaid, forgotten
like the promise
of a better future
of any future
of hope

of repetition
a parody of some impossible
finality, the possible:
a voice trailing off
into the sky
like wisps
of smoke from
the delicate cigarette
left to smolder
in a red plastic ashtray.

I feel as if I
have left something out...

---

* *Ty Cronkhite teaches composition and English Literature at a community college in Greeley, Colorado.*

Sonnet Regarding Buttons

Twere buttons all about her, head to toe.
Of them she knew nothing, hidden as they were
to her dim thoughts of what she ought to know.
Yet they were there as sure as sure is sure.

To Steven it was always very clear.
Most were plainly labeled, color-coded,
fastened by the wire to some noxious fear.
He faced a quiet cannon day to day.

This one makes her happy, that one makes her mad.
Green one on her forehead is for crazy.
Blue for joyful, mauve for nice, gray for sad.
Press them all at once: transcendental hazy.

In her state of emotional undress,
what button now will Steven dare to press?

JACQUELINE CHOU

An Ode to Jammie Evans

This was back in the '70s. Jammie was in my fifth grade class, and he lived in the same building of the Exterior Street projects as my best friend, Melanie Wilkins. His name wasn't pronounced 'Jay-mee.' It was pronounced 'Jammy,' like eggs cooked perfectly over medium, the yolks golden-orange, slightly firm and creamy. I don't know if it was just a nickname, but that's what everyone called him, even the teacher.

We were all poor, but Melanie and Jammie – they were a different kind of poor than I was. They were regular, black poor, you know? Working class blacks. There wasn't a lot of money, but enough. Melanie was always nicely dressed; her mom made sure of that. Mrs. Wilkins straightened Melanie's hair with those iron clamp contraptions once a month, and then styled it in cute hairdos every couple of days – curled bangs and variations of ponytails. Sometimes a single ponytail in back; sometimes one on each side of her head. Sometimes it would be one ponytail with all Melanie's hair brushed all to one side. Always with those elastic hairbands with the colorful plastic balls at the ends. Melanie's ponytails were always all nice and poofy, like a black girl's hair could be. And she usually wore some polyester button-down shirt, all swirly with some psychedelic pattern, with a color-coordinated sweater vest over it. Melanie looked like *style* to me.

Me, I was a different kind of poor. Welfare poor.

My mother, three older sisters, and I lived in the unfinished basement

* *Born in New York City, Jacqueline Chou studied Philosophy and Comparative Literature at New York University, where she also completed an MA in French Literature and taught French. Her stories have appeared in a number of digital and print literary journals. She lives in New York City.*

of a house on Bailey Avenue. It was one very large room, cold, with walls of stone, and a concrete floor. In one corner, there was a minifridge, and round wooden table with a hot plate on it. Five mismatched chairs encircled the table. That was our kitchen.

The other end of the room was the "bedroom," which consisted of blankets and pillows that my mother got from the Salvation Army, all spread out on the floor in a square area of around ten feet. That's where we all slept. We had a miniature old-fashioned TV set up in one of the corners of the blanket area. It was mostly static, but you could make out the pictures enough. Channel 7 came in the best, and this was good, because we loved to watch Charlie's Angels and Starsky and Hutch.

We were on food stamps, and ate poorly. And my mother got our clothes secondhand from the Salvation Army and Goodwill, so we also dressed poorly. Wednesday mornings were class assembly for me, and I had to wear a white blouse and blue trousers. The best my mother could find was a white blouse that was worn-looking, and yellowed. It was too small for me and the buttons strained down my front. The blue trousers were the right size, but they looked old, too, and the button at the top of the zipper was missing. My mother put a safety pin on it.

I would look at myself in the long mirror that my mother hung in the bathroom. Me in my welfare clothes. I was embarrassed to go to school like that, but I had no choice. Being that poor creates an ever-present anxiety. You're always embarrassed and afraid. You're always embarrassed because you know your clothes are funny. You're always afraid of the unknown: the teacher is going to say you have to buy something for a project, or you were going to need money for a class trip.

Christmas season brought on an additional level of anxiety. All the kids in class would talk about what they wanted for Christmas, what their parents were going to get them. My sisters and I didn't get Christmas presents. When the other kids talked about what their Christmas lists, I couldn't tell them what I really wanted, more than anything else: normal, store-bought clothes, and Pro Keds sneakers, like everyone else had. I really wanted Pro Keds badly, so the mean kids wouldn't make fun of me for wearing "skips." That was the derisive term used for the cheap sneakers that you could buy in Alexander's Department store back then. Sneakers piled high in a plastic bin, each pair held together with a plastic band looped through the shoelace holes.

So in the Christmas season, I would prepare my lies. Lies that I would tell the first day back after Christmas break. I would think of what to say that I got for Christmas. Three Mini-Mod dolls! They looked like Barbie dolls, but they were better, because they had way more outfits. A giant Hershey's Kiss. What else? Was that enough Christmas presents to pretend that I got? I thought I had to add one more. Bubble-gum scented bubble bath. My list of fake Christmas presents was complete.

Why was Melanie friends with me, I'm sure I did not know. In addition to being noticeably poorer than everyone else, I was the only Asian kid in our grade. Melanie was so pretty and cute, and while she wasn't in the popular group, the popular girls liked her. Maybe Melanie liked me because she and I were the smartest kids in class, and we were both funny. Yes, I remember I was considered funny back then, though for the life of me, I can't recall a single joke I made back when I was ten, and I don't even remember what makes ten-year-old kids laugh.

But best friends, we were. After school, we would go to her apartment in the projects – it was always her house, not my place. I used the excuse that I suppose most poor kids use when they don't want anyone to see their home: "My mother doesn't like my friends coming over."

And sometimes I'd see Jammie Evans, because he lived on the floor just above hers. He was goofy-looking. Skinny, gangly. His eyes were bulgy, and he wore black horn-rimmed glasses. His skin was the color of coffee with a little milk in it – a dark shade of cappuccino, I guess. His smile was wide and bright, with crooked teeth. He had big feet and neon orange shoelaces in his Pro Keds.

Every class has at least one weird kid, and ours was Jammie. He had no friends. At lunchtime, he would sit at the end of one of the long cafeteria tables, eating his hot school lunch all alone. He didn't seem to mind, I think. He'd just stare off into space, sometimes looking around. And he'd chew his food slowly, so deliberately. When the cafeteria served hot dogs in buns and beans on the side, he would use his spork (do they still call them that – the plastic hybrid of the spoon and the fork?) and scoop up all his beans and pile them on top of his hot dog, a sloshy mess that made the hot dog bun all wet.

"Eww, lookit. Jammie's fucking up his hot dog again."

That was Eric Gonzalez, calling out from the other end of the cafeteria table. Eric was one of the popular kids, and the popular kids *cursed.* Everyone would look at Jammie at the far end of the table, all by his lonesome, placidly chowing down on his hot dog-and-beans sandwich.

"Eww!" a bunch of kids called out. "Eeeewww, look at Jammie."

But Jammie didn't react. He kept chewing, placidly looking over at the catcallers, his bug eyes not blinking. And he wouldn't say a word. When we all finished eating, we'd all go out to the school playground for the remainder of lunchtime. The boys would play dodgeball or softball, and Melanie, the other girls, and I would just stand around talking, or play jump rope. That was the only sporty thing I was good at. I couldn't jump double-dutch, but I could jump in and out without missing a beat, never stepping on the rope.

Jammie, he didn't have anyone to hang out with. He'd just walk around the perimeter of the schoolyard fence. He had a loping walk, and his arms would swing back and forth. Like a giraffe with arms. Around and around he'd walk, until lunchtime was over. Sometimes, he'd reach his hand out, grazing his fingers over the chain link fence. When he passed by us, I could hear him singing to himself.

I noticed him, but I never thought much about him, you know? None of us did.

One Saturday morning, Melanie and I were supposed to go over to the library together. We were going to work on our reports for Heroes in the American Revolution. I was supposed to meet her in front of her building, but when I got there, there were already two teenagers there, hanging out at the benches that were a couple of yards from the entrance. The scary kind of teenagers. Loud, laughing and cursing. I wanted Melanie to come down quickly.

The teenagers saw me, and the shorter one called out, "Ching Chong, Paddy *Wong*!"

And he lifted his index fingers to the outer corners of his eyes, and pulled outward, turning his eyes into little slits.

"Ching chong, ching chong," he repeated. His friend laughed.

My ten-year-old body backed up, pressing against the wall of the building, my head tucked down. I was only four and a half feet tall, but

I couldn't make myself small enough to be invisible. I kept very, very still, like a rabbit hiding in the wild. It didn't work. "Ching chong, ching chong." The other teenager joined in his friend's game, and started to approach me. I just wanted them to leave me alone.

And then I heard a voice alongside me.

"Want a Twizzler?"

I looked to my left, and there was Jammie. He must've just come out of the building. Those eyes behind the gleam of glasses peering at me. I looked up to meet his gaze – he was so much taller than me, then looked at the teenagers in front of me. Jammie turned and looked at them too. His expression never changed. Placid, open. I think Jammie only had two expressions: blankness, and a broad grin. Right now it was the blankness. Exactly the same expression as when he looked up from his bean-covered hot dog and everyone was screaming, "Eeeewwwww!"

He looked back at me again, an outstretched hand that was holding an open package of Twizzlers. I pulled out a red braid-y stick from the package. "Thank you, Jammie." Jammie nodded, and pulled out a Twizzler for himself. And he stayed right next to me, both of us nibbling wordlessly on the firm chew of the licorice.

The rhythm of the teenage boys' taunting had been broken. The boys looked at us, this unlikely pair of bespectacled black giraffe-boy and bespectacled and impoverished little Chinese girl, standing there eating Twizzlers. They seemed embarrassed.

"Come on, man. Let's go," one said to the other. And with that, they wandered off.

We watched as they reached the end of the block, and disappeared around the corner.

Jammie waited maybe a minute more, then said. "Okay, bye."

"Okay, bye," I repeated. I watched, perplexed, as he walked away, in the opposite direction of the teenage boys. What had just happened? Jammie's presence made the older boys stop. Had Jammie done it on purpose? He must have. It had all happened so quickly, and Jammie was so weird. Something happened at that moment, even if I didn't realize it right then and there.

Jammie Evans now had a special place in my heart.

* * *

The school year went by quickly, and it was suddenly June. The anxiety of the last Christmas was a distant memory, and the dread of the next Christmas was in an equally distant future. But there were other terrors for the financially stressed.

The summer carnival. The ferris wheel! The spinning teacup ride! The cyclone! Milk bottle bowling, ring toss, water gun games. Cotton candy, candy apples, and popcorn, all set up in the athletics field of JFK High School.

All of those things cost money. Mrs. Wilkins was going to give Melanie five dollars for the carnival. That seemed to be the standard amount that parents were giving their kids. Days before the carnival, I had asked my mother for carnival money. My mother pulled out her purse from the handbag that she had made from an old pair of denim jeans. She carefully withdrew some money from the purse and placed it in my outstretched hand. Four shiny quarters.

That familiar feeling weighed me down: a sinking in my stomach, accompanied by fear. I was going to run out of money before Melanie, and everyone else. I was dreading it. I wished I could just move away, or get sick, or it would rain that day, and the carnival would be cancelled. But I pretended to be excited about the carnival. I lied and told Melanie that I was bringing five dollars, too. Readying myself, I prepared a fake scenario where I would lose my pretend five dollars as soon as we got to the carnival.

The day of the carnival I met Melanie in the lobby of her building. She was carrying a laundry basket filled with dirty clothes. "Come with me. My mom wants me to put this in the wash before we go." So we went inside, and took the elevator to the basement. Down the dark concrete hall with the fluorescent lights. When we entered the laundry room, there were two people already there. There was Jammie at the folding table, with a pile of laundry and a big plastic bin. And there was an older woman who was just settling a laundry bag on the floor, next to the jumbo washer.

"Hi, Mrs. Penn."

"How ya doin', Melanie."

"Hey, Jammie," I said.

"Hey."

Mrs. Penn placed a big pile of quarters on the washing machine. It made a big clattering noise. Then she jolted, and made a clicking sound with her tongue. "Won't get far without detergent," she muttered to herself. And she hurried out of the laundry room.

Minutes had passed. Jammie had just folded the last of his stuff and put in his basket. He wrapped his arms around it, and walked out of the laundry room. Melanie had her back to me: she was splitting the colors and whites between two washing machines. Mrs. Walker hadn't returned.

That big pile of quarters gleamed under the fluorescent light. I don't know if I even thought about it. I took a big step over. My hand was like the claw in the crane game that they would have at the carnival: it dipped into the pile of coins and grabbed a whole bunch. I panicked at the unmistakable sound of coins jingling as I put them in my pocket, and looked over at Melanie, but she hadn't turned around. She was busy pouring single boxes of detergent into each washer.

We were out the door moments later, my hand still in my jeans pocket wrapped around the coins, making sure my quarters didn't make any noise.

* * *

The horror of my crime made it impossible for me to enjoy the carnival. My stomach was already a roiling pit long before our seats on the Ferris wheel reached the heights of the sky. The cotton candy and popcorn were nauseating, seasoned with my overwhelming guilt. I couldn't even finish them, and I threw them out. All I wanted was for carnival day to be over. I just followed Melanie around until she was ready to go. We passed by Jammie as we were leaving the field. He was standing in front of the water-squirting game. He must've won big, because the guy in the booth was handing Jammie an enormous stuffed alligator. Around three feet long, fur of the brightest of greens, except for its white underbelly.

Jammie looked so pleased, holding that thing in his arms, his face bearing his biggest grin.

"Hey, Jammie."

He looked at me and I was on the receiving end of that joyous smile.

And he walked half with us, half behind us, back to Melanie to the projects. I was going back with Melanie, because her mother had a sweater she wanted to give me.

When we got to the lobby, I froze: Mrs. Penn was there, and gesturing angrily to a big man that I had never seen before. Tall, wearing a bus driver's uniform. Mrs. Penn turned around at the sound of the door opening. A bolt of lightning shot through her arm, and she pointed at Jammie.

"Him!" She looked back at the big man. "Your son, Jammie Evans. He stole my laundry money." The big man looked at his son, and at the stuffed animal in Jammie's arms. That was apparently all the confirmation he needed.

"Jammie, you apologize to Mrs. Walker." Jammie just stood there with his enormous alligator. He looked back and forth at the woman, and then to his father, his glasses gleaming as much as the ever did.

Silence.

"Goddam, Jammie." Jammie's father stepped forward, and slapped Jammie across the face. Jammie's let out a cry of surprise and pain, and protest, too, because Jammie knew full well that he didn't steal that money. A millisecond later there was a cracking sound: Jammie's glasses went flying and hit the mailboxes.

Melanie tugged my arm. "Let's get out of here."

The ding of the elevator reaching the lobby sounded behind us. We turned and rushed toward the elevator door.

"Damn, Jammie," Melanie muttered as she pressed "Eight." "How could he do something so stupid?"

I couldn't answer. Just before the elevator doors had closed, Jammie turned his head toward us. Face stripped of its glasses, he was squinting. I couldn't tell if he was looking at me, but my heart was pounding. The sounds of Jammie's cry, the crack of his glasses hitting the wall, rang through my body.

On Monday at school, Jammie had a swollen lip, and one lens of his glasses had a crack in it. I wanted to run over to him to tell him I was so sorry, that it was all my fault, and I didn't mean for it to happen. I could never bring myself to do it. I avoided Jammie after that, turning my head away whenever our paths crossed. I never learned if he got his father to believe him, that he didn't steal Mrs. Penn's laundry money. I wondered if Jammie knew that it had been me.

The end of the school year came, and then it was summer. I would see him once in a while in the project's playground, and I would always avert my eyes. Fall came, and mercifully Jammie and I were put in different classes: I, in Mrs. Gutterman's, and he, in Ms. Lopez's. I would see him now and again throughout the years. Ever tall and skinny and quirky, yet somehow majestic to me.

The thing about being poor and Asian in the 70s – and maybe even now, I don't know – there were chances to make things better. Last year of junior high school, we all took the test for the special high schools. I scored well, and made it to Bronx Science. Did well there, and got a full scholarship to New York University, and got a master's degree in social work. All this to say that I ended up doing okay. Not rich, but okay. More than okay. That impoverished, desperate kid that I had been is many lifetimes ago.

I had to go to the old neighborhood today. First time in over twenty years. I was assigned to a case of a woman who had just left the shelter for abused women and was settling in a little apartment on Bailey Avenue, with her two young kids. My meeting ended early, and I had some time to kill. I walked, passing P.S. 122, and its fenced-in schoolyard. Several blocks more, to Sedgwick Ave. I stood for a long time in front of that old house, where me and my mom and sisters lived in the basement, all those years ago. Something tugged at my heart, as I remembered us, a poor Chinese woman who spoke pidgin English, with her four little girls in that cold cellar apartment.

I then started towards Broadway, toward the projects where Melanie used to live. Some delicious smell wafted through my nostrils. I sniffed in deeply, trying to identify the scent. I looked up and saw the banner flags and a sign that said, "Grand Opening! Taqueria Fonda. Free soda with lunch."

It was packed inside, but that didn't deter me. The smell of carnitas was too enticing. The line was long, and there were people leaning against the walls on either side of the line, waiting for their food. I looked up at the illuminated menu that hung above the front counter. Carnitas tacos, I thought to myself. And guac and chips. And then someone started yelling.

"You people don't know how to run a business. I've been waiting for twenty minutes."

My eyes followed the voice. A man of medium height, wearing a white button-down shirt with the sleeves rolled up. He was leaning over the counter, leaning his face into the face of the Mexican guy on the other side.

The counter guy, gave him a smile, broad and solicitous. "Dentro de poco. Soon!" His accent was heavy. He quickly went to the soda case that was alongside the counter, pulled out a can of coke, and handed it to the yelling man. The man took it, but kept continued yelling.

"I'm *supposed* to get a free soda." He pointed to the sign outside. "Lunch. Free soda. That doesn't make up for making me wait twenty minutes. Do you even know what your own sign says?"

The counter guy kept smiling, but he looked embarrassed. "Soon," he repeated. The man was relishing the counter guy's discomfiture.

"Do. You. Understand. What. I'm. Saying?"

I wanted to punch the guy.

Mercifully, a second worker came through the swinging door from the back just then, carrying a plastic bag. The counter guy looked so relieved. He checked the receipts on the bag, and said to the angry man.

"Camarones?"

"It's about time," he said, grabbing the bag.

Thank God it was over. But no.

The guy didn't leave. He just kept yelling.

"You know, it's people like you that come to this country, and don't even realize what asses they are. They don't learn the language, and they open stores ..."

The counter guy still had that frozen smile on his face.

"And they don't even do things right. You need to learn the language. Have a little respect for this country. You can't keep someone waiting for twen –"

"You got your food, now get out."

A low voice cut off the angry man in mid-sentence.

The angry man spun around, and tilted his upward to look at a tall man behind him.

"What did you just say to me?"

"You got your food, now get out."

Stunned, the angry man just stood there.

"Get. Out."

The Angry Man was now Embarrassed Man. Without a further word, he walked out of the store. Someone actually started applauding. The tall man turned around and watched.

Horn-rimmed glasses covering big eyes.

Is that Jammie Evans??? My heart started pounding.

With the angry man gone, the tall man turned back to face the counter.

The guy at the counter raised a bag of food at the Jammie lookalike.

"Free! Free." He was smiling, a genuine smile now. His eyes tilted upward to meet the eyes of the tall man. His eyes were bright and soft with gratitude. "Free," he said again.

I saw the tall man shake his head, reach in his back pocket and pull out a money clip. The ding of the cash register, a brief exchange of coins and bills. I watched as the tall man turned to leave. Familiarity washed through me as he passed by me. I stared at his back, the baggy fit of his salmon-colored oxford shirt as he walked out. I fought the urge to run out the door and go after him.

Just stay put, I thought to myself. *You don't even know for sure if it's him.* But an involuntary force overtook me.

"Excuse me," I said, jostling the woman behind me.

"Excuse me," I said to the gentleman behind her.

I pushed past several more people and rushed out the door.

In the bright sunlight, I looked to my left, and then to my right.

I saw the tall figure in the salmon shirt, nearing the end of the block, heading toward Broadway. Fuller now, but still quite slim. Those dangly, swing-y arms, one hand carrying a bag of Mexican takeout food.

"Jammie!" I cried, my voice ringing all the way down the block.

The man stopped and turned around. And then he looked directly at me.

It was really him. Twenty-six years later, there he was. I waved at him. He didn't move, his expression unchanging. I had never known him well, but I just witnessed what I had experienced all those years ago. Jammie Evans stood up to the bullies and protected the little guys. This unassuming guy was an unnoticed hero. All those years ago, he protected me. All those years ago, I had wronged him so terribly.

That man on the corner remained still as I walked toward him.

I quickened my pace, as thoughts flurried in my head. Should I ask him out to dinner, so I can confess to him the terrible thing that I had done, all those years ago. Or should I just blurt it all out on the street corner, as soon as I got close enough? I didn't know what I was going to say. There was one thing I was certain of, though.

Perhaps it wouldn't matter one whit to him; perhaps he wouldn't even remember who I was, but I was going to give Jammie Evans, this steady, slow-moving train of human decency, this patron saint of the put-upon, a long-overdue apology.

MARCUS DELMONT

Three Days

For three days, we lived in the house of strangers. My wife says I should be grateful. I am grateful. But I am also many other things I do not have words for; not in their language, not even in my own.

We met the man outside the Red Cross building in October. The cold night air pierced our bodies. We did not have thicker coats. In Berlin, I told Farzana to leave them, telling her it was warmer in Belgium. She called me a fool; she was right. A Red Cross worker pointed to us, sitting on the cold pavement with our small suitcase. The man walked over, smiling. He said something I did not understand, but I took his extended hand. I told him my name was Mohammad. He shook Farzana's hand. She could at least greet him in his language. His eyes lingered on her too long. My wife is beautiful and intelligent. She had been training to be a pharmacist. That is how she knew some English words. But it is no longer possible for a woman like her to exist in Afghanistan. There is no word for the shame I felt.

We followed Thomas home on the underground train. He was polite, but he spoke too much, kept smiling at my wife. I prayed we would only stay one night.

He lived in a building of flats. The lift smelled of anxiety, probably my own. But when he opened his door there was life. A little boy greeted us. A small dog sniffed my shoes. A woman smiled and shook our hands. There were toys on the floor. I smelled cumin and garlic. Though I could not comprehend her words, I understood they had prepared a meal. Suddenly, I remembered I was hungry.

** Marcus Delmont is originally from Rhode Island, USA. He has lived in Brussels for 18 years, currently in a quiet corner of the city with his family and two dogs. He is a new writer, and this is his first publication.*

At their table, the man laid down a fragrant pot. He pointed to himself. Farzana whispered that he had cooked. I tried to nod politely, but Farzana pinched my leg. I could only understand one word he said: *shorwa*. He served me rice and a stew that looked like shorwa, but my mouth did not recognise it as shorwa. It was weakly spiced and in place of lamb were white blocks, like sponges. I looked at Farzana. She was eating and smiling, but I knew she was eating without pleasure. Her eyes told me to obey. So I ate this shorwa with the white blocks.

Soon, the man brought out a tablet, onto which he typed quickly. He was using a translator. The Dari was not correct, but I understood that he apologised because he wanted to make us a meal from our home, but he used tofu instead of lamb. Though I could read these words, I did not comprehend. I kept eating and used his translator to thank him.

Any anxiety felt between us was melted away by their son. He was three years old. His cheeks had dimples so deep that I wished to bury my fingers in them. After dinner, we played on the floor with him, building with his blocks or watching him talk. Farzana's smile was as bright as a full moon, but it was the smile of loss.

My affection for this family grew during the next two days. They took us shopping. In a busy store, I chose a black leather coat, the kind I had seen men in Berlin wear. The woman was displeased and spoke to her husband. Farzana told me to put it back, but Thomas took it and shrugged before paying. Later, we spent time in a park. The boy had a football. We kicked it back and forth until the sky turned dark blue.

At their home, Thomas declared through his tablet that he would cook shorwa again. I told Farzana to help him in the kitchen. While she did that, I showed the boy football videos from my phone. From the kitchen I heard Farzana's laughter, the sound of a knife on a cutting board, the pop of evaporating liquid. When dinner was set, Farzana winked at me. I was prepared for the sponge blocks, but the feeling in my mouth was not that – it was of home. Cumin and coriander; turmeric. Pieces of carrot, some onion and garlic. And lamb. It was still nothing like my mother's shorwa, but it was enough for me to ask for a second plate. I mustered my courage and looked the man in the eye. In his language, I told him it was good.

And this is how we spent many hours at the table, typing on his tablet translator and pinching his son's dimpled cheeks.

The next morning, the woman from the Red Cross called me to say that we should go to the immigration office. A place had been found for us. I told Thomas through his tablet. He smiled, but it was also a smile of loss. I know, because it was my smile too.

A few hours later, I hugged his son goodbye and touched his fine blond hair. Thomas's wife hugged me. Even their little dog came to say goodbye. Farzana's eyes told me she wanted to stay. But I told her to leave. This is our life now: always leaving.

Thomas ordered a taxi to the immigration office. No one had the courage to speak. The taxi stopped in front of a tall building. Thomas pointed to the door. By now I could understand the words thank you. He gave me an envelope. Immediately I returned it to him, but he insisted. He embraced me, then Farzana. His eyes were wet. I held his hand and with my words, I expressed to him a gratitude which he could not understand but which I hoped he could comprehend.

We were on our own again. But you know, even in distance, separation, and longing, there is still love. Even as the taxi drove away.

MERYL A.H. FRANZOS

Hair of the Dog

BEEP...

"Are you on your way to your friend's?" Matt's voice called out from the phone.

"I'm stopping at the store, and then I'm there," Nyoko said, reaching into the Pump N Go's beer refrigerator. She felt a rush of cold air on her face and collarbone.

...BEEP...

"I'm sorry your sister did this to you – us – but no loose ends, right, babe?"

"I'll know what I'm dealing with soon."

...BEEP...

"Nyo, you know how much winning this seat in the Florida House means to me, right?"

"Uh huh." Nyoko pulled out a can of Miller Light.

...BEEP...

"And our pasts do not equal our futures, as long as–"

"There are no loose ends," Nyoko replied. "Got it, Tony Robbins. Talk to you later."

...BEEP...

It was morning. BEEP... 11:59 a.m. BEEP... morning-*ish*. BEEP... Nyoko stood in line at the Pump N Go, hungover in Ojibwa, Michigan, while a scraggly man held his SNAP card at the ready, rocking on the balls of his feet... BEEP... and the lone clerk individually scanned twenty-five or so bottles of grape and orange soda... BEEP... Nyoko moaned, head throbbing, guts churning... BEEP... God, she just wanted to get herself right... BEEP... but... was that scraggly man... Cody Becker?...

** Meryl A.H. Franzos is a Hapa Californian, born and raised, but currently hangs her hat in Pittsburgh. She misses the ocean and Ranch Style Beans.*

BEEP... *Holy Christ, it is!...* BEEP... Back in high school, he'd been a bad boy with a speedboat – short, slick black hair, and blue eyes so icy he looked like a husky you wouldn't leave a baby with... BEEP... He jetted around Ojibwa Lake with his backwards cap and his iridescent Vuarnet sunglasses... BEEP... There was always a girl in a bikini on his glittery teal boat... BEEP... He even took her, Nyoko, for a ride when she first moved to Ojibwa... BEEP... Nyoko slunk behind the yellow beef jerky display and continued observing... BEEP... But now Cody looked like Forrest Gump during his running phase – hair and beard long and streaked with gray... BEEP... disheveled clothing... BEEP... a deranged, half-vacant look on his face... BEEP... It was sad, really... BEEP... Not that her life wasn't sad... BEEP... Two weeks ago, she had been under the knife getting the revirginification surgery Matt wanted. Meanwhile, her bipolar sister was holding an illegal garage sale at their parents' estate... BEEP... Nyoko's life was sad in a different way.

"Should I swipe my card now?" Cody asked, far louder than needed. His once raspy and articulate voice had become atonal and slow.

"Bombs away, m' dude," said the pimply-faced clerk in the red Pump N Go smock.

Nyoko blanched while Cody carried his bags of drinks outside – in two trips – limping as he went. Maybe she was wrong. This couldn't be the same person.

"Bye, Cody Becker! See you in a couple hours!" the clerk said, waving after him.

Guess that's all cleared up. She set her Miller Light on the counter and dug through her quilted Chanel tote for her wallet.

"Loosy to go with your hair of the dog?" the clerk asked.

"No, thank you."

Thirty seconds later, she was outside amid the oppressive buzzing of cicadas and the Tractor and Feed store's corporate banjo music echoing across Main Street. The sun hung directly overhead, bathing everything under its auspices in unforgiving light. Dark, ghoulish shadows under everyone's eyes. Small marooning islands under cars and fueling canopies. Nyoko found a sliver of shade near her rental car, next to the ice chest and propane exchange locker, where she sat on the curb, her head and torso in the shade, her legs and feet in the sun, nursing her hangover with small feminine sips to avoid the burps. If she burped now, it wouldn't be pretty; pretty was the way her fiancé liked her best. *It's what you practice in private that you will be rewarded for in public*, is what Matt, or one of his motivational speakers, would say. She rolled her eyes until the sound of rushing liquid drew her attention over to the air pump (FREE O FOR SOME GET UP AND GO), where Cody was pouring out a grape pop, and when empty, he shoved the bottle in a dirty pillowcase. He repeated this thirteen more times, hissing CO2 and tinkling soft drink, until the grape was exhausted. Then the orange pop. All of it on the asphalt. Not one sip passed his lips. It was both mesmerizing and perplexing. The last bottle of orange pop glugged out, joining where the rivers of purple and orange had blended into a brown, shimmering estuary of high fructose corn syrup.

Just then, the full bore of Cody's pale eyes settled on her, catching her in a stare. She sat frozen, locked in his vacant gaze, her teeth chattering, while she waited for a flicker of recognition, and for those black pupils of his to blot out his irises. But if he knew her, it did not register on his face. He turned and shuffled across Main Street with the bulging sack slung over his shoulder. It was as if she had made eye contact with a ghost.

She chugged the rest of her beer (burps be damned), hoping to drown her mounting panic attack. She tried to meter out a low belch, but it turned ugly. The beer came gushing out between her Lanvin flats, still cold, frothy like dog sick. She could pretend to be, strive to be, pretty all she wanted. But deep down, she still felt as ugly and dirty as that day on Cody's boat eighteen years earlier. She could still smell the Armor All on the vinyl, could still feel the burn of carpet nap under her butt, could still see through tears the winking teal sparkles on the bow of the rocking boat.

Just then, a text message buzzed in, jolting her out of the past. She drew her phone and a tin of breath mints from her purse.

Jessica Dykstra wanted to know: *We still on for lunch?*

Nyoko popped three mints and considered postponing. She'd never hear the end of it from Matt if her middle-school and high-school diaries weren't back in her hands at the earliest opportunity. He'd already made it abundantly clear that this loose end, among her hundreds or maybe thousands of other loose ends, was the most important. "They are historical records that can harm me – I mean us," Matt had said. Nyoko chucked her beer in the nearby trash and typed her response to Jessica: *Yep. On my way. Just running a few minutes behind.*

Nyoko drove through quaint downtown Ojibwa. She motored past Cody, limping along with his dirty pillowcase. For some reason, the thought of running into Cody again hadn't crossed her mind, which was odd, considering how ridiculously small the town was. Population: six thousand. She chided herself for letting her guard down. After six blocks, Main Street became M-28. Town turned to asparagus fields, then rolling green hills dotted with cows. It wasn't long before she spotted the Dykstra's Dairy sign, followed by three enormous white barns and an equally enormous white farmhouse.

Jessica Dykstra née DeKryger waved from the porch. Her auburn hair flashed red in the sun. Six feet tall in ballet flats and built like a Dutch warrior princess, Jessica was burly enough to wrestle a Holstein (which by virtue of being the wife of a dairy farmer, she often did). They'd first met in seventh grade. Nyoko was drawn in by Jessica's kindness to her as the new kid – the only Asian in a lake of white – but it was Jessica's wicked sense of humor and capacity for teenage mischief that kept them friends. After a big hug, they walked through a screen door that closed softly behind them and settled in the kitchen, at the corner of an ancient farm table, with mugs of coffee and plates of Amish coffee cake and grilled cheese between them.

Jessica stirred cream into her coffee. "Gosh, I haven't seen you since..."

"My mother's funeral," Nyoko finished her sentence. Three years, two months, and twelve days ago.

"I'm so sorry I couldn't be there for your father's in April."

Nyoko waved her apology away. "You had the stomach flu. How have you been since?"

"In all truth, it wasn't stomach flu." A smile crept onto Jessica's face, and her hand fell to her abdomen. "We've been trying to start a family. It's... well, we've had a lot of trouble for many years, but... We are expecting! My first trimester was 'the never-ending morning sickness story.'"

The obvious questions fired out. *When are you due? Do you know the gender? Names picked out?* She only half-listened to Jessica's giddy answers, while a burgeoning sense of her own motherlessness and childlessness pressed behind her eyeballs.

"Enough about me!" Jessica said. "What's happening with you?"

"The wedding planning and dealing with my parents' estate is all-consuming," Nyoko said, keeping it surface, "as is Matt's campaign for state senate. But of course, we're still finding time to be active in our church and the pro-life movement."

There was a flicker of something in Jessica's eyes – judgement, probably – but she was diplomatic enough not to press. They settled on local gossip, specifically, as it turned out, Cody Becker.

"I just saw him at the gas station..." Nyoko said. "What happened to him?"

"Oh." Jessica's eyes bulged. "Cody was in a terrible boating accident a couple of years ago."

"A boating accident!" Nyoko said.

"He made quite a name for himself racing. But I guess he had some demons. One day, he had too much to drink, went too fast, lost control of his boat, and *bam!* Right into the marina."

Nyoko scrunched her face.

Jessica continued, "And now he's dane bramaged and living with his mother."

"Geez," Nyoko said, eager to change the subject. "Any other small-town gossip?"

"Unfortunately, yes." Jessica pursed her lips. "There's a rumor going around that your sister has a drug problem."

"It's not a rumor." Nyoko sighed and felt the itch to drink herself blotto all over again. "I just got her checked into rehab yesterday. Now to close out the estate before Ayumi steals any more of it."

"Such a shame... I still can't believe she put your diaries and journals out in her sale. Glad I was there though." Jessica clucked her tongue as she walked over to her pantry.

"Thank you for calling me when you did." Nyoko pulled her purse onto her lap and fingered the benjamins in her Chanel wallet. Matt had given her five thousand in cash, in case silence had to be bought

– anyone who'd read the journals could blab to the press, ruin Matt's campaign platform, Matt's dream. *Their* dream.

Jessica emerged from the pantry with a yellow gift bag in hand. "Your juvenilia, my dear."

Nyoko peered inside; the bag contained all the familiar floral covers of her diaries and story journals, even the small Hello Kitty one that held the most dirt. "What do I owe you?"

Jessica wrinkled her nose. "Nothing, Nyo. Get out of here with that talk." She resumed her place at the corner of the farm table, her back to the eight-burner stove.

"Well, thank you for not letting these get into the wrong hands," Nyoko said, holding Hello Kitty tightly. There was stuff in these books that even her high school BFF didn't know about. (And hopefully still did not.) Nyoko's insides squirmed. "Did you read them?"

"Just enough to confirm what they were." Jessica dropped her voice to a whisper. "Don't worry, I won't tell a soul that you got to third base with Jonah McDaniel back in the day." Jessica cackled and elbowed her in the ribs. "*Oh, Jonah's fingers strummed me like he strummed his guitar*."

"Cut it out." Nyoko could feel the blood flooding into her face. "Did you read them or not?"

"No," Jessica said, looking affronted. "I know we haven't stayed in the best contact after high school, but I think of you often."

"You do? Why?"

"Sometimes I go running in Oak Glen Cemetery. I check on your mom's grave and remove the weeds and leaves from time to time. The pictures you post on Facebook are just stunning. I wish they were here to see what a lovely bride you will be."

The blood drained from Nyoko's face as rapidly as it came. That she was even thinking someone who tended her mom's grave would take hush money was the ultimate cosmic check. Especially someone who thought better of her than her own parents did. *What did you expect would happen? You should have known better!* Of all the things her parents had said during her first summer in Ojibwa, these two statements hurt the most. Two tears rolled off her cheek and splashed onto her jeans. Nyoko laughed, sputtering a little while she tried to reverse the tears back into light-hearted conversation, but failed when a full-on sob hiccupped out of her.

Jessica reached over and rubbed her back as a good mother would. “Coming home brings back a lot of sad memories, huh?”

“Something like that,” Nyoko said. “I should get going.”

“So soon? You haven’t even touched your lunch.”

“I need to check in on the auction house people.” Nyoko stood up, dabbed her eyes, and blew her nose into an American flag napkin. “I’m trying to get the house on the market, close out the estate. You know, put this all behind me before the wedding.”

“Well, if you need help, or a hot meal... don’t be a stranger.”

“Careful,” she said, “I just might take you up on that.”

“I hope you do.”

Nyoko sped back into town, windows down, sunglasses on, and Matt on speaker phone. He was finishing up his morning at the American Cancer Society walkathon when she told him the good news. “I have all my journals and diaries. Jessica doesn’t know anything. Wouldn’t accept any money either.”

“Hey, that’s terrific, babe!” Matt said, “Hooo-eeee! What a relief!”

She laughed as the tension between them thawed a bit. For the past week, she’d felt more like a liability or a task on his to-do list than his fiancée. As she crossed the town limit sign, she slowed down, rolled up her windows against the humidity, and turned on the air conditioning. “I wish you were here, Matt... Some of this... It’s harder than I thought. I ran into Cody–”

“Babe? I have to run and do some ‘grip and grins’ just now, but why don’t you make a nice bonfire later tonight with those diaries and call me?”

“Oh, okay... Bye.”

Nyoko pulled into the Sav-On Groceries lot and parked near the cart corral. She killed the engine and punched the steering wheel as she exited. Possessing her diaries still wasn’t good enough for Matt. She jerked a cart out of a stack and wheeled it toward Sav-On’s outdoor displays: cords of firewood, bins of watermelons, pallets of Kingsford Original charcoal. It was almost like he didn’t trust her with her own past, which was ridiculous. And if it was so important to him, why wasn't he here? Obviously, with the election, he didn't have time to get caught up in the estate stuff, but still. He could've come for a day or two. He could at least not expect her to erase all of it.

She'd just loaded her cart with firewood and a quart of lighter fluid from the Summertime Dealz display when she rolled up on Cody Becker feeding his bottle collection into a computerized deposit kiosk near the store's entrance. Stupid small town. He was bouncing, excited, like a child about to get some candy. Nyoko flipped her sunglasses onto her head and rubbed the small area where her brow met her nose. It was humbling to think of all the hours of her life she'd spent fearing him, building him up to be some blue-eyed boogeyman. Now he was basically the town idiot. *Or was he?* She veered her cart close and said, "Excuse me."

Cody spun around as the kiosk spat out a receipt.

"You just bought and dumped all of those drinks out an hour ago," she said. "What's your end goal?"

The outer edges of his pale irises were lined in navy, and the extreme contrast between the two colors made him look both startled and predatory. She felt herself flinch.

"I'm transferring money to a high-interest account," he said.

Nyoko scrutinized the kiosk. The digital total on the machine read $2.50. She calculated in her head. "A five-cent on the dollar return? Does your mom know you're doing this?"

"Don't tell my mom." His wiry shoulders tensed under his 2007 St. Clair Classic Offshore Power Boat Race T-shirt. For a second, the hairy, disheveled man in front of her was a sixteen-year-old boy again. He was scared of his mother back then, too. "Please, don't."

"I won't," she said, taken aback, "I was just–"

Cody ripped the bottle deposit slip from the kiosk and limped through the store's automatic doors, leaving her to explain whatever she was doing to herself.

Nyoko entered the store in a huff, grabbing supplies at random – toilet paper, a twenty-four-pack of Michelob Ultra, a handle of Tito's vodka, club soda, a roaster pack of chicken, and a bag of limes – until she spotted Cody at the customer service desk. The Sav-On's employee placed two bills and some coins in his outstretched hand. He left while she was queuing at the check-out. The irony of their changed positions loitered uncomfortably, but she chased it to the far reaches of her mind and locked it away. Why should she feel concern for him? She rubbed the nape of her neck. Or worry if his mother abused him as a child, maybe even still did? He'd robbed her of so much, even the love of her own family. *Fuck him*. If her parents had taught her anything, it's that vulnerability shouldn't be protected; it should be exploited.

She cruised Main Street, scanning for a particular loping gait on the horizon until she spotted her quarry. Cody was heading south, back towards the lake. It was a long walk from his mom's place to the Pump N Go to Sav-On's and back – about nine miles round trip. Nyoko slowed alongside him, her heart thrashing in her chest, as she prepared to do the opposite of every screaming bodily instinct.

"Cody!" she said from the open passenger window. "Need a ride back to the lake?"

He turned to her. His eyes could still freeze the very breath inside her lungs. "Can you take me to the Pump N Go?" he asked.

Nyoko smiled. She knew it was more of a baring of teeth, like a scared dog. Talking to him on the street was one thing; inviting him into her car was another. "Sure. Hop in."

The passenger door slammed, and the scent of Tide mingled with fresh sweat. He smelled just like the day on the boat. They rode in silence. A mounting panic attack crawled up her trachea and wrapped its hot tentacles around her brain. She pulled into the Pump N Go lot with black stars firing at the edges of her vision. She blinked, and they were coasting into the parking space near the ice chest. She hit the brakes. The car recoiled slightly when the bumper tapped the yellow stanchion.

"I'll be right back," Cody said. "Don't leave yet."

Gasping, she watched him limp into the store. Then the rearview mirror, where the shiny asphalt buzzed with yellow jackets. The hypnotic side-to-side dance of the insects held her quietly until Cody opened the door and sat back down next to her, and cracked into a tall boy wrapped in a brown bag.

He sat upright, guzzling his beverage until his vacant expression transformed into a manic grin.

Nyoko swallowed the flutter at the back of her throat and said, "You like beer?"

He nodded, like it was the only thing on earth that gave him any relief. She knew what that was about. No. Stop humanizing the monster. "What kind did you get?"

He peeled the bag away to reveal a silver can that read Steel Reserve. "This one is cheap, but good. And there's a lot."

"You bought it with the cash from the pop bottles?" she asked.

He nodded again, and this time the lines around his eyes widened to meet his smile in long crinkles. "My high-interest account!" he said, laughing in loud nasal ha-ha's.

Nyoko cocked her head sideways. "I don't understand. Why didn't you just buy a beer instead of all that pop?"

Cody downed the rest of his Steel Reserve and belched. "Can't buy beer with SNAP cards. Not allowed." He rocked himself now and appeared to be suppressing a smile (but not very well).

"Ah, but you found a way, didn't you? You bad boy." Nyoko forced a laugh and wagged her finger at him. "Still, it's an awful lot of work for one beer."

"It tastes better when I take things," he said.

At this, Nyoko stopped smiling, feeling a sudden coldness come over her. "Time to go home."

They drove with the windows down, past the middle school, and turned onto Lake Drive, heading west around the lakeside community neighborhoods.

"Cody, do you know who I am?" she asked, as they passed under a grove of Jack Pines.

He shook his head slowly as the tree-filtered light scattered across their arms and faces. "I was in an accident. Thoughts don't stay in my head, and I don't remember things... Stop up there. That's where I live." He pointed ahead at a pink and white Swiss-style chalet that needed fresh paint.

She already knew. 7027 Lake Drive. Just four houses away from her parents' place. She pulled into the driveway. The dock and boathouse sat beyond. Without the sparkly teal speedboat bobbing in the water, the buildings looked as vacant as his face.

"You shouldn't get into vehicles with strangers then," she said. "It's not safe."

***

Nyoko drove her father's boat – a newer fiberglass Chris Craft with teak accents – around Ojibwa Lake in a slow evening cruise. The water reflected the brilliant red sky, now fading to the color of a ripening plum as the day edged into twilight. Sunset was a good time to share and reflect on the day with those you love, even if they were a thousand miles away, like Matt.

"He's basically Jesus at this point. Innocent as a newborn lamb." Nyoko killed the engine in the middle of the lake. "Heck, he's even performing miracles!"

"Turning Fanta into beer is not a miracle. Food stamp fraud is a despicable crime," Matt said. "Were you thinking about confronting him about your rape?"

"I don't know," she said. "I guess I wanted him to know all the things he took. I wanted him to know how it felt when my parents chose him over me, when they refused to press charges. They literally said, 'Why should we ruin the young man's future, when you should've known better?'"

"Geez..."

"But will screaming at a disabled person bring me the retribution I think I'm due? No. So I need to figure out another way to get closure." Nyoko grabbed a beer from the mini-fridge, popped it open, and took a long drink. "I vote accidentally-on-purpose running him over with my car."

"Well, little miss, don't do that! But if you vote for me, I'll make it my life's work to get rid of food stamps. Then where will he be?"

"Ha-ha," she said humorlessly.

"So, what are you going to do about your dad's boat?"

"Don't change the subject."

"Maybe we could bring it down here, where we could enjoy it together?"

"Good God, Matt, no! Boats are holes in the water in which you pour money." She paused and took another drink. "Even the auction house wouldn't take it. I'm only out here to make sure it runs, and it does.

Tomorrow, I'll list it in the Pennysaver, and hopefully it's gone by next week."

"Alright, alright," he said. "It was just an idea. Have you disposed of your diaries yet?"

"No..."

"Don't you think you should do that ASAP?" Matt said.

"I was talking about what *I* need!"

Matt let out a deep sigh. "Cody can link you to the one thing my constituents get up in arms over. What if confronting him jogs his memory, and he becomes a liability? Doing nothing is awfully convenient, don't you think?"

She noted the darkening sky. She noted that the boat had drifted into the desolate and marshy end of the lake. She noted that even the waterlilies had folded back into themselves and closed up for the night. "I know, but–"

"Nyo. I gotta run. Joel's been waiting for me inside the bar."

"But you're the one who's always telling me to identify the problem, but give power and energy to the solution – *Help me find a solution!*"

"I know you'll do the right thing, babe. You are in my thoughts and prayers," Matt said, before hanging up.

Nyoko let out a tortured shriek that scared the nearby waterfowl into flight with a collective snap of wings. The heavy bass of their departure reverberated across more than just the lake. She cruised back, using the beer to stave off the loneliness while she abided Ojibwa Lake's after-dark five mph low wake rule. By the time she secured the boat at the end of the dock, the Teapot constellation had emerged in the night sky.

She hated being needy. She could feel her need repel him. Need repelled strength. Strength attracted more strength. She had to be strong for him, but not *too* strong, because he didn't like that either. It was hard to get the ratio right. The dock boards clacked hollowly as she carried the bag of diaries to the firepit. Maybe once she did what he'd asked, the expanding space between them would collapse and throw her back into his good graces. Maybe the cleansing power of fire and the figurative erasing of her past was all the closure she needed? She had to try.

Apple wood and Pennysaver doused in lighter fluid ignited like magic.

Incendio! Within minutes, the inferno settled into a solid bonfire, and between sips of beer, Nyoko fed her diaries into the flames. First, the blue calico journal. The fabric cover bent and curled outward while a thin orange line chased the ivory off the pages. When it was black and crispy, she lowered the red calico journal in. Then the mauve paisley. The teal brocade. The black and white speckled composition books. Until at last only the shiny red Hello Kitty diary remained. Nyoko thumbed through the pages. August 1992.

...Just when I thought my summer couldn't get any worse after being raped, I am now seven weeks pregnant...

...My parents made me tell him he has to pay for the abortion. I wish I was dead...

...Cody visited my father at the end of our dock tonight and handed him $1,000 in cash. Apparently, it's all the money he'd won from boat racing this summer because he didn't want his mom to know. My dad gave him a beer...

...I got an abortion in Kalamazoo today. I start at my new school in three days. I doubt seventh graders can be meaner than my own mother, who has been referring to me as 'that slut' ever since I confided in them...

Nyoko tossed the diary into the pit, wishing all these memories would disappear from her head permanently. *Obliterate!*

"What are you doing?" Cody's loud, atonal voice asked, as he limped across the last of the Van Houten's property and onto her brick-paver patio.

Nyoko jumped at first, then stared into the bonfire. The glossy cover with Hello Kitty's white head and red bow boiled up and exploded. Goodbye Kitty. She shook her head slightly. Who was she kidding? There would be no erasing, no forgetting, no closure.

"Nothing," she said. "Just lessons in futility."

"What happened to the old man who lived here?" Cody asked.

"He died."

"Oh." He shuffled uncomfortably.

"Why, did you know him?" With her opposite hand, she aimed the bottle of lighter fluid at the fire and squeezed until the flames whooshed up and the bottle sputtered. She tossed it aside and finished her beer.

"He took me out," he said, glancing at the boat, "let me drive sometimes."

The empty beer can fell from her hand. "Did he now?"

"Gave me beer too," Cody said, staring at the empty can on the ground.

Really Dad?! Tears were at the threshold, coming. She thought about driving out to the middle of the lake and drilling into the hull of her father's boat until the water poured in, and just sitting in it while it sank into the darkening blue. If anything would make him flip over in his grave, it would be the desecration of his beloved watercraft. Nyoko clutched her head, bracing against the sharp-as-ever betrayal, when an idea grabbed her, jolting her out of her seat. The firewood snapped and crackled. The flames licked the sides of the stone fire ring.

"If my father were still alive..." She smiled at her own private joke. "He'd never forgive me for being a terrible host. Would you like a beer?"

"Yes." He dragged an Adirondack chair up to the fire.

Nyoko clambered into the boat, grabbed two beers from the mini-fridge, and paused a second to clear her head. Was she capable of this? And was it what she wanted? The din of crickets and the touch of a cool breeze was a tempering contrast to the roar and heat of the fire. Her mind had never been clearer. *Please, Lord, let me have this.*

She handed Cody two cans. "So, you like speedboats?"

He nodded and popped a tab.

"Do you like to drive fast?"

He sat forward at the very edge of the lounge chair and nodded enthusiastically. His curly mop of hair bobbed with him.

"I heard you used to race boats." Nyoko licked her lips. "Do you remember?"

Cody looked deep into the fire as if he'd hoped to find something there. The flames put artificial life into his eyes. After a minute, he sank back into his chair, shook his head no, and drained his beer. "Sometimes I remember things when I drink."

"Then keep drinking and remember." Nyoko grinned and lowered her voice. "Because my father wanted you to have his boat."

"Heh-heh-Haiiir?!" Cody stood and pointed to where the boat's name, Hair of the Dog, painted in blue cursive and outlined in 24K gold, bobbed in the cone of the green light at the end of the dock.

"Shh!" Nyoko motioned for him to sit down and be quiet. "Yes, 'Hair of the Dog'... but of course, your mother would never allow it, right?"

Cody collapsed into his chair. His face crumpled. Moms are forever the ultimate fun-busters. "How then?"

At that moment, a chunk of firewood rolled over, and the last of the Hello Kitty diary crumbled to the bottom with the ashes of her other journals. Nyoko stood and collected her garbage. "I'm sure you'll figure something out."

"Wh-Where are you going?"

"Don't worry about me. You stay, drink, enjoy the fire." She glanced out to the boat, where the keys dangled from the ignition and glinted in the moonlight. "There's more beer on the boat if you run out. Goodnight, Cody."

She walked up the gentle slope of green towards the house, turning back now and then, willing the night to swallow him.

* * *

The next morning came quickly. She cleaned herself up, put on her white floral dress and straw sun hat, humming as she went. Avoiding the windows facing the dock. Avoiding her phone. Avoiding her thoughts. She headed to Sunday services at the Church of the Holy Redeemer, taking the long way around the lake, the one that didn't go past Cody's house. Avoiding. Still, there was something in the air this morning. Something that made the fine hairs on her arms stand and her lizard brain wriggle.

Her Sunday morning drive came to an abrupt halt near the town beach. In between the woodland pines and the sun refracting off the water, Nyoko spotted a long furrow of overturned earth and some mangled steel playground equipment. Soon, this partial view was obscured by municipal buildings. One by one, the cars in front of her did K-turns, pushing her up to the front of the traffic line where a solitary cop in Oakleys stood amid the yellow tape and white sawhorse roadblocks. Behind him, fire trucks and flashing emergency vehicles surrounded the local soft serve joint, The Lakeside Swirl. She thought of many summer evenings spent at this park. Perfectly pulled half-

and-half cones – top-heavy and luscious, bound for tragedy – passing through the small takeout window. Sticky asphalt. The peeling rubber sound the soles of her tennis shoes had made against it. She grabbed a bottle of Purell from her purse and rubbed the harsh gel into her hands. The cop twirled his finger and pointed, signaling her to turn around and head in the opposite direction. The detour made her late for church.

ERIN GAURA

Bed Linens

It was three in the afternoon, but it may as well have been nine in the evening. The sun was tucked behind layers of velvet curtain clouds that cast a cool grey haze, the shade of the old monastery's crumbling stone that marked the western edge of the town, forming a boundary between civilisation and the unforgiving mountains. Their peaks of exposed stone reached out from their grass-covered bases and disappeared into the mist. The streets were emptied save for a figure silhouetted by a lamp outside the train station. Its fluorescence illuminated a nylon hood, the water off which cast a halo. Moisture gathered and clung to the ends of the hair that framed her face.

Idle, incomprehensible chatter drifted from inside the train station. She slung a black canvas rucksack over her shoulder and stepped into the shade of the afternoon, and suddenly she was washed over in greyscale. She walked along the town's main street – arguably its only street – the exposed plastic on the worn-down heels of her boots clicking as loud as horseshoes. The streets were usually vacant in less-than-ideal weather, but she thought, gratefully, that it was more desolate than usual. She was rarely alone when she ventured through town, and now each step, which she took to counting, seemed to ring in her ears. Boarded up beauty salons and cobblers lined the road; a solo operating news agent; one long obsolete pub, its name printed in peeling lettering; two pubs with their doors flung open inward, beckoning; and one dual-use pub-and-undertaker, a relic of the lucrative business of pint pouring and body burying of previous centuries. She didn't think the undertaking services advertised were much more than a facetious attempt at nostalgia for the townsfolk who still saw the town through rose-tinted glasses.

---

* *Erin Gaura lives in Galway, Ireland.*

No sooner had she started on the road when she arrived at the town's only apartment complex: twelve units contained in a dull block with too few windows and painted a despondent shade of pale yellow. The entrance to her apartment was ornamented with a mat, a relic from the previous tenant, and a pair of work boots crusted with days-old mud. Her keys clanked against the door and the lock rolled with an audible thump as she opened it.

He was not there, not sprawled across the couch, the news not playing to an absent mind. His things were still there, proof of his former presence: a record player, a raincoat, his collection of books dating from his schooldays to a few months ago. A tin of his specific brand of coffee on the counter. His favourite mug, a gift from his niece's school trip to Paris, left upside down in the dish rack.

She pressed the bedroom door ajar, and turned the light on in the bathroom. Having resolved herself to the silence and the singular toothbrush in the cup on the sink, she wandered back out into the kitchen. The rain picked up and rapped aggressively on the slanted overhead windows.

She wondered if she should take the photos from display on the bookshelf. Were they memories seized by some divine hand and stamped on paper, or leering reminders that everything went wrong? She held the faded Polaroid from a friend's birthday party, captured within her arms around his shoulders and his right arm around her waist as she leaned backwards, laughing at something unremembered, his gaze cast downward in a half smile at the drink he held in his lap. It was tucked into the frame of another photo of them at his sister's wedding in Spain. She remembered the intense, unrelenting heat of the August sun, and his parents taking the photo at their hotel before leaving for the chapel: a rustic, one-room building scarred by the Spanish Civil War. She had taken her sunglasses off for the photo and in the sixty seconds to take it, the sun boiled the wetness in her eyes. Tears beaded at the edges of her squinted eyes and he said, 'Jesus, it's a wedding not a funeral!' Or something along those lines, faded now, and the squint that was captured emerged from the corners of her mouth pushing the apples of her cheeks into her eyes. In his face, she still saw hers, though she had searched his features in recent months and found no traces of herself, nor did the chord of his voice reflect the tune she remembered. She left the photos as they were. The jolt that ran through her still left the heat of the Spanish sun on her muscles.

The quietness draped over the apartment created a void in the room unlike the silence she came home to when he was still at work. The rain hammered at the window. She absently switched on the television. The news anchor stared at her, delivering the facts of some latest atrocity, but with the woman's measured cadence filling the room, she felt less alone. Mechanically, she set about putting away the coffee, the mug, emptying her backpack. She was neither performing the actions nor listening to the news but suspended in the abyss between. The usual modicum of untidiness that followed him had disappeared; even the bin was emptied, and the sink was scrubbed. Was she to change the linens on the bed now? Would sleeping on his scent when he was no longer around be as alien as sleeping in a stranger's bed, or would she rouse in the night tireless after having found herself alone?

She boiled the kettle, but it was cold before she poured it over a tea bag. The water turned a feeble shade of grey as she watched the bag wheeze its essence into the liquid. From the cabinet, she pulled boxes of cereal and baking supplies. Her arm, swallowed by the cubby, reemerged with half a bottle of red wine crowned by a maroon-stained cork. It was bought five days earlier, before she left to stay with her parents. She didn't normally keep alcohol in the house, but he had gone that night and her nerves were as taut as a bowstring.

She poured a small measure into an oversized wine glass, drank it in one go, then filled it to the nearly invisible 175 millilitre mark. Even with the hum of the news still resonating, the apartment rang hollow, and she felt as though she were in some remote cabin, far removed from even the tiny village. The view of the looming mountainside eclipsing her window in inky black did not help. The phone rang, reminding her that she was never fully alone in the 21st century.

"He's not here, Catherine," she said before the voice on the other end could get a word in.

"Did he get the car looked at?"

"I don't know. He's not here. He moved out, remember?"

"I thought you might have spoken to him."

“I haven’t.”

“Don’t you think you ought to?”

“No.”

The line was silent. Catherine’s first time without an opinion.

“Is there anything I can help you with, Catherine?” She rubbed the tiredness from her eyes and dropped onto the couch sideways, pooling onto the cushions with her legs over its arm.

The old woman sighed audibly, blowing static through the microphone.

“Aren’t you worried about him?”

“I am always worried. That’s why I can’t have him here anymore.”

“If you talk to him, tell him to ring me.”

“If he’s not answering, try the pub.”

She hung up before another intrusive question. She contemplated blocking the number but decided it to be too cruel. Catherine meant well, despite having trouble with boundaries. It was her generation, her rural upbringing, her lack of experience outside the village where everyone knew each other’s business.

She watched the news ticker roll across the screen without reading its words. She switched off the television, the red strip still lingering in her vision against the black backdrop. There was a purple stain in her glass where the bowl met the stem and she swirled the parched drop around. Would she move or would she get used to claiming their shared apartment as her own? Catherine’s words, aren’t you worried, dug a hollow in her chest and planted themselves there. She was more worried than ever – with him gone where she couldn’t keep her eye on him and where the future was uncertain. Her death grip on authority dug its nails into the edges of the cavity excavated by Catherine’s words.

Aren’t you worried, she asked herself. No, she responded. It was hard to pretend in such an obvious lie. Where was he now? He was not hidden in the darkness out the window, even though she didn’t expect to find him there. He was staying with a friend just on the outskirts of town until he had a more permanent plan. But without being there, she may as well have been in another universe, another timeline. Gone but traces of him embedded in every corner of the apartment. His curly hairs were stuck to her sweater, tangling with wool and her own long ones. The last record he listened to was still on the platter of the record player; she didn't look to see what it was. The table had a scorch mark at the centre where he once left a candle burning until it extinguished itself. He was everywhere, even where he wasn't. He wasn't there, but she saw him as he busied himself in the corner, at the table, with books. She decided she needed to change the bedsheets.

KEVIN MACALAN

Wish You Were Here

At a quarter to four, a timid knock on the bedroom door disturbed Liam's summer night. Still cocooned in a fuggy damp, he forced himself out of sleep and recognized his father's apologetic face. It hung palely from dressing-gowned shoulders. With fists clenched to his chest, his father exhaled a few words.

"I can't breathe."

The hospital made Patrick comfortable ... for a few days.

Shortly after, Patrick gave up a struggle he'd sustained for a long time. He left during one of Liam's rare absences. It was the first time Liam could remember Patrick doing anything Liam hadn't wanted. Liam handled the situation, efficiently, but coldly, somehow outside himself, and certainly without company. He buried his father on the fourth of July; the day Liam might have been celebrating Patrick's sixty-sixth birthday, but no.

For twelve years Patrick had lived with Liam. Twelve years since retiring from Alanstown Council on the grounds of ill health. The same twelve years during which Liam had been building his banking career. During that time, Liam had never taken a day off work to accompany his father to a cricket match or even taken a long lunch to meet his father for a pint. Admittedly, cricket was an unusual passion for an Irishman, but who couldn't find time for a pint? No, Liam had hurried through twelve years of life, chasing, always chasing, and now his father had gone. What, exactly, had he been chasing?

Two days after Patrick's birthday, Liam bought stamps at the village post office.

"How's Patrick?" asked the postmaster.

"He died," spat Liam, swallowing hard. He reached for his stamps

---

* *Kevin MacAlan lives in rural Ireland. He has an MA in Creative Writing.*

and change. The coins refused to obey his fingers. After a pause, Liam raised his eyes a little, but not enough to meet the postmaster's. He shifted his weight in the silence of the empty post office. "He ... he was ill. Then he died."

"I had no idea," the postmaster cleared his throat. "No one told me. He was always so cheerful. He was in a couple of weeks ago, still talking about going to the West Indies."

"Yes, for the cricket," said Liam. "I never understood his love for the game. But, no ..." Liam turned to leave. "He died."

At the door, Liam faced back towards the counter. The postmaster was still in position, as if expecting more, or as if only the glass partition prevented him from reaching out. Liam's mouth opened, but remained silent. His face burned with tears. He gnawed against a bolus of nothing and felt the absence of his father in everything.

That Friday morning, at ten-thirty, Liam noticed the phone ringing and decided he would answer. He moved into the hall and sat on a dining chair by the telephone table. A telephone table! Patrick had insisted on a landline. Never had that man owned a mobile phone, written a text, or read an email. Liam remembered the iPhone he had bought Patrick for his sixtieth birthday. He pulled open a small drawer that fitted the curved polished features of the dark wood table. There was his father's iPhone. Still boxed. Sun shone starkly through lozenges of stained glass in the front door. The phone continued to ring. Liam lifted the receiver.

"Liam? It's Cormac; Cormac O'Brien from the office."

"Cormac."

"We need to talk, Liam. It's been three weeks. We need medical certificates or something. Can you come into the office?"

"No, I ... don't think I can."

"Liam, can I come to you?"

"Yes. Ok. Next week, I'll call."

Liam replaced the receiver very gently. He ran the palm of his right hand around the bristles on his chin, and felt his face warm and wet. He closed the telephone-table drawer, pushing his father's phone out of sight. Rising to his feet unsteadily, he was overcome by the effort, and he lowered himself once more, this time to sit on the floor among a pile of letters at the foot of the front door.

Mesmerized by the rich tick of the grandfather clock, he looked at the stairs where nobody stood. His breathing hushed. Each pendulum fall sounding more and more like the impatient tap of bony fingers; irascible Death, out of sight but waiting.

Between each second, Liam unpicked the orchestration of near silence around him. The faint rumble of traffic, so distant it spoke of being elsewhere; the birds scampering on the flat roof of the kitchen extension; the relentless drip of a bathroom tap. He tuned his ears to the faintest sound, the drone of the electric immersion heater, and heard water molecules excited by the heat moving in the tank, wrapped in insulation, hidden in the hot press, closed in the back bedroom, upstairs. He could hear the air motionless in the attic. And he thought, for an instant, that he heard breathing. Then, inches from his face, the phone caterwauled madly. He snatched the wire and ripped it from the wall.

The next Wednesday he shaved. Bearded, he looked like Patrick. It was a clammy afternoon, and he lowered the roof of his Golf Cabriolet for the ten-kilometer drive into Alanstown. He left the top down when he parked; a departure from normal practice. After an hour or so, the world seemed very normal. He bought fresh fish for tea, enough for two, but he knew what he had done. He restocked his freezer, but bought fresh vegetables as well, and fruit; plenty of fruit. He threw the groceries into the back seat, and turned the radio on as he drove out of the city, past the cemetery. At home he sorted through the mail. All those for Patrick he marked 'no longer at this address' and set to one side. All for him, he binned.

That evening he put Patrick's letters into a rucksack, cheerfully donning the bag, he walked half a mile to the post box near the Tavern Inn, and returned them all to the mail. The empty bag he threw into a large waste bin at the back of the pub. He entered the snug, and ordered a double Jameson and water.

"Oh, and a packet of plain crisps," he added.

"Have you been away?" asked the barman.

"No."

"Only I haven't seen you since I got back from Spain."

"No, I've been here ... Well, at home."

"How's Patrick?"

"Oh. Well ..."

"Good."

"No. I don't mean 'well'. I mean ... Well ... I mean you wouldn't have heard. Actually he isn't well, he's ..."

The barman put down the glass he was polishing, shocked by Liam, who stuttered on for a little longer but soon fell incomprehensible and slumped across the bar. A green beer towel darkened in the moisture of his tears. The oak counter muffled his sobbing. The barman rested a hand on Liam's back and called for help. Liam's whiskey remained untouched.

In the morning Liam stayed late in bed. From there, he could see each of his mother's postcards, which lined his bedroom wall. Liam's mother had died the year before Patrick retired. Liam's university chaplain had given him the news of her accident. Her second husband, Tommaso De Luca, died with her, and it was the De Luca family who arranged the funeral. It fell conveniently during a mid-term break – a break Liam would normally have spent with his mother. His routine, and his mother, somehow remained intact. She was buried in Palidoro, near Rome, but since his summers in Italy were due to end anyway as his working commitments began, as far as Liam was concerned she lived on, albeit at an unreachably distant place.

Her postcards, each one a different scene from Italy displayed at a jaunty angle by one corner stuck firmly behind the painted picture rail, each had a brief message of fulfillment written hurriedly on the back. He no longer needed to read them. A glance at the picture was enough for him to hear his mother speak the words from its back. Sometimes the image mixed with the sentiment, a 'bye for now' in Rome had a bustle about it, quite different from Venice. Each card had the immediacy and vitality of the moment they were written. These were moments he still had.

A determined thumping on the front door pulled Liam from his bed, but only as far as the front bedroom to spy through the blinds down at his visitor, Cormac O'Brien. Instinctively, Liam dropped to the floor beneath the window. He breathed shallowly in fear of detection. By the time it occurred to him that the thumping had stopped, he was also aware of being seated at the foot of his father's bed. He had no recollection of making it, but there it was, neat and angular. Its clinical regularity had no depression in the mattress, no softness in the pillow or ruffle in the covers indicating human contact, but it did have an air of expectation. Patrick's bed had not lost hope.

Some while later, when Liam was throwing away rotten fruit, he noticed how long the lawn had grown – too long for his own mower to cope. He drove to Dungarvan to a tool-hire company and rented a petrol mower. He used Patrick's car because it had a larger boot, and as he struggled in the street to load the mower into the car, he was aware that a man he had never met before watched intently.

"You must be Liam," the stranger said. "Where's Patrick then?"

Liam didn't look up from his struggle. In fact, he closed his eyes. He shut them, and his ears.

He put himself as far under the canopy of the car's open boot as he could. He fumbled busily, angrily, with the mower, pushing it into his own-created darkness, into the furthest recess. Short of breath from the effort he turned slowly to the stranger.

"He's ..." Liam let out a resigned sigh. "Erm ... He's in the West Indies."

"Good on him!" said the stranger.

Liam composed a smile. "I must get on," he said. And he left.

The drive home was too short and Liam motored into the country, unable to find roads that remained unfamiliar for long, but enjoying a great sense of discovery in every long bend of boreen. He imagined Patrick's white beard contrasting with the sun-darkened dapples that appeared on his cheeks and forehead each cricket season. Patrick sprawled restfully in a deck chair, and watched half a dozen West Indian kids playing cricket on a white-sand pitch. The murmur of a breeze whispered through palm-tree fronds and gentle waves pushed rhythmically at the beach-cricket boundary, occasionally rolling over the outfield and levelling the sand to receive fresh imprints of naked feet chasing a well-struck ball. Patrick sipped a drink and tipped his hat lower over his eyes.

The next day, Liam returned the mower without having cut the grass. He joined the motorway at its junction just outside Alanstown and, for the first time since losing his father, drove north towards his office.

"Liam?" Cormac O'Brien's secretary appeared more embarrassed than surprised. "We won't bite," she said, sensing Liam's uncertainty and asked him to take a seat while she went to ask Cormac if he could be seen. Cormac made himself available, but seemed equally embarrassed.

"If it's about the dismissal, it's too late to ..."

Liam interrupted, without aggression. "Dismissal?"

"Yes, we've written several times ... given notice that we needed documentation, discussion, anything ..."

"You've sacked me?"

"You didn't know?"

"No ... I said I'd call ..."

"That was in July!" Cormac stood up from where he had sat behind his desk. He picked up a pen and toyed with it as he paced around the office. Calmly, he added, "Look, we're all sorry about Patrick ..."

"Dad?"

"Yeah, he ..."

"What's this got to do with dad? Dad's in the West Indies."

"But I thought ..."

"No, Cormac, you didn't think ... None of us ever do. If we did, then we'd all take a leaf out of dad's book and live while we can."

"Patrick's in the West Indies?" Cormac sat down, not behind his desk this time, but in one of the low armless chairs arranged around a small circular coffee table. He threw his pen into the seat opposite and let out a long-frustrated sigh. "Personnel I think," he strained. "Or was it Tom from the cash desk? Oh, I don't know who it feckin' was, but somebody, definitely, told me Patrick had died."

"No. Dad's in the West Indies, and I'm going to join him. I came to resign, but it seems you've done that for me. I'll be in touch."

More than a week later, Liam was anxious that he had no postcards from Patrick. This anxiety was prompted by a shop in a small arcade off Alanstown's Main Street that hung a bold sign in its window saying 'This is not An Post.' The narrow shopfront displayed glass-fronted cases filled with first-day covers and stamps, and boxes of postcards, old and new. Similar items burgeoned from cabinets and stacks of drawers inside the shop filling every cramped inch. Set to one side, towards the back of the counter, a box of postcards marked 'West Indies – Various' came to Liam's notice.

Two days later he showed a postcard to Mrs. Wilkinson, a friendly lady who lived near the pub and kept cats. She was enormously large, with a bosom that stood before her like a tabletop beneath her sagging chins. She wore a checked coverall permanently, and found bedroom slippers the only comfortable footwear. She was rarely seen beyond the flower borders of her own front garden, but Mrs. Wilkinson knew a lot about the village and Liam thought it likely she believed Patrick dead.

"Why's the corner torn off?" she asked.

"I'm sending the stamps to a friend's son," said Liam. "West Indian stamps are particularly colorful."

"He hasn't signed it."

"Well, you don't, do you, postcards? Sign them, I mean. You just scribble them and send them off in a hurry."

Mrs. Wilkinson handed the postcard back to Liam as if it were an unwanted gift. She smiled. Her smile said, 'I'm not convinced,' and Liam spoke cheerfully about her cats instead, making several endearments rhetorically, and rapidly, without pause. He bid her farewell.

Liam stepped into the public bar of the Tavern Inn – it was disappointingly empty. The landlady herself kept bar. This time, Liam placed the postcard on the counter as he ordered his Jameson and water, but the landlady didn't comment, and Liam chose not to draw attention to it. He ordered a second drink, which he downed in the time it took the landlady to bring him his change, and a rush of swagger freed him to speak.

"I got a card from Dad."

"A card?"

"Yeah, a postcard. Look ..." Liam proffered the picture side, his thumb obscuring the torn corner, but his momentary bravado had slipped, and the landlady appeared to be looking at him rather than the card.

Eventually, Liam did find someone he could tell about Patrick's trip to the West Indies. Tomás Kelly was a retired farm laborer who had taken to cleaning windows to subsidize his pension. He wasn't very reliable, since he lived some distance from the village and didn't always cycle so far out on his round. He hadn't called since June, and probably for this reason had lost most of Liam's neighbors as customers. Unusually, Liam asked him in to do the inside of his windows as well. There were several postcards to exhibit, each with a torn-away stamp, a brief message of fulfillment, and no signature. Tomás's only query was in reference to the rest of Liam's mail, which was accumulating into quite a heap by the front door.

The next day Liam bought stamps he didn't need. The postmaster asked if he was feeling better. Liam took a long time to reply. As before, he avoided the postmaster's eyes and shuffled uneasily, but today he spoke calmly, apologetically.

"Mr. Murphy ... Actually dad isn't dead." The postmaster made no comment. Liam continued. "I ... I just made that up, you see. Dad did go to the West Indies, like he always threatened ... er ... planned. He had to go, or so he said, because the next time he was ill might be the last time. But I didn't want him to go ... I'm sorry."

"But Liam, you were so broken up ..."

"Yes. Yes I was, because he deserted me, you see. We'd had a row about me following my career to the grave. Dad said he couldn't wait any longer, he wasn't getting any younger."

"Wasn't?" The postmaster picked up on Liam's choice of words.

"Oh right! Isn't ..." Liam corrected. "I feel really ashamed now, but at the time I wanted him dead ... So I could forget him."

"You don't want to forget him, Liam, just learn to live with his memory."

"But I don't have to. I have cards from him, as I have from mum ..."

"Liam! Listen to what you're saying. Your mum's been dead a long time."

"Oh yes, I know ... But dad isn't. Believe me, you'll see. Dad's in Port of Spain, Trinidad, watching cricket and supping Bacardi."

"For the cricket, is it?" Postmaster Murphy shook his head, either confused over Patrick's death, or his love of cricket.

After this, Liam stayed at home as much as he could. Mr. Murphy's look of benevolence haunted him. When Cormac O'Brien called, Liam hid once again at the foot of his father's bed until he heard Cormac's footsteps fade away down the path. Liam drifted into the kitchen, aware of a hunger, and there stood Cormac at the back door, his eyes fixing Liam with a chilling seriousness. Although Liam momentarily considered pretending Cormac wasn't there, Cormac himself opened the door and stepped into the kitchen, so Liam remained and acknowledged him.

"Cormac. How nice."

"I'm sorry to barge in, but your mobile is dead and your home phone just rings ..."

"It's unplugged."

"And you haven't responded to the bank's settlement letter. They're offering redundancy ... It's quite generous."

"I'm a bit behind on my correspondence. No stamps."

"Liam. I ..."

"Cormac?"

"I've spoken to people in the village, Liam. They're concerned for you. You're ill. They know Patrick died. You yourself told the barman at the Tavern Inn, and your man at the Post Office, so you know it too. But then you told me he was in the West Indies."

"He is ..." Liam moved as if to usher Cormac back through the door.

"Now you even claim to be getting postcards. Liam, Patrick's dead. It's very sad, but you must keep a grip on reality."

"No, Cormac. Look ..." Liam marched into the lounge. Cormac followed closely behind, almost struck by Liam when he turned waving a fistful of postcards.

"These postcards," asked Cormac. "Where are the stamps?"

"I send the stamps to ..."

"No, no you don't. You tear the corners off the postcards because they have no stamps, because they have not come from the West Indies, or from your dad, because your dad is dead. They're not from him, are they? They're not even signed ..."

"Ok, ok," Liam paused. He remembered the day in the pub; the last time he felt this loss. "I can't do the signature." He leaned forward onto the writing desk taking his weight on his left arm. Cormac moved closer. Liam's head stooped, his right arm hung limp for a while, then pulled open a drawer filled with blank postcards and scraps of paper covered in failed attempts at Patrick's signature. "I can't do his signature."

"Oh Liam," Cormac moved closer still. Awkwardly, he raised his arms and, at first just touched Liam's shoulders gently, but as Liam broke into a sobbing rhythm, Cormac pulled him closer and held him tight.

"You must force yourself back into reality," Cormac said, handing Liam a cup of coffee. "It's no good shutting yourself off. You have to plug in the phone, open your mail. You need help, but you have to help yourself as well."

"I don't know what I was doing," Liam sipped his drink and waited for the shakiness in his voice to subside before continuing. "I lost track. It's like you step off the conveyor to catch your breath, and when you're ready to get back on, everything's gone so far past you've lost the way back. I wanted to convince myself I was alright by convincing others, but ..."

"Will you cope?"

"Maybe. It's been a while... I guess I feel more stupid than anything."

"Alright, so where do we start?"

"What do you mean by 'we'?"

"I'd like to help, I feel partially responsible. What about that mail by the front door? I bet your settlement offer's in there somewhere. Can I look through it?"

"Be my guest."

Cormac moved swiftly whilst the offer was available. He brought an armful of mail into the lounge and started sorting it into piles. At first he hummed while he sorted, but fairly soon he fell silent. He became more fervent in his actions as if looking for one particular type of thing in Liam's mail.

"Liam," he asked. "What are these?" In his hand he held a wad of postcards, each with a particularly colorful stamp, a brief message, and Patrick's signature.

"Sorry we argued," said the one on top, "but I'm not getting any younger and my next illness might be my last. You have to live while you can. Wish you were here."

SCOTT MACMANN

A Child's Christmas in Ohio

President Nixon bombed Hanoi for Christmas when I was eleven years old. But the indelible marks of that holiday season, which burn in my heart to this day, do not involve Nixon.

Not much.

In my memory, I was in my upstairs bedroom, sitting at the window desk – ice crystals obscuring my view to outside – scribbling the first lines of "The Heroic Adventures of Star-Captain Bill Wehman on Mars."

Downstairs, my big sister's shrill shrieks rose in battle with the assembled adults. Not wanting to miss this, I set aside my literary ambitions and crept down to the bottom of the stairs.

Her voice quivering, she gestured with practiced theatrics towards the nicotine-stained ceiling. "Cousin Stevie is dead. He's dead."

One of our uncles replied, "He's not dead."

"He's dead, and you're watching football." She put her hands to her face and sobbed. "Like animals."

I poked my head around the wall to see the full room. Ten aunts and uncles, plus our parents, sat squeezed into our tiny living room. Beer cans and bottles were everywhere. Lit cigarettes and ashtrays were, too. Dad snored, oblivious. Mom, holding a cigarette and a beer bottle, stared at her daughter.

Opposite the adults stood the hallowed television, and in front of the TV stood my sister.

"Who's Stevie?" I asked.

Sis turned towards me and pulled her hands away from her face.

** Scott Macmann is a writer, editor, and publisher living in Cincinnati, and currently serves as President of the Cincinnati Fiction Writers. His novel Militopia will be published in 2026 by Dragon Street Press.*

"Who's...? Our cousin, you idiot. How can you be so stupid?"

"He's not dead," said a different uncle. "He's just shot down."

My sister wheeled around. "From fifty thousand feet? He's dead. And you all killed him. You voted for Nixon, and he killed Stevie for you."

"I didn't vote for Nixon," I said. Technically, that wasn't true, since my sixth-grade class had voted unanimously to re-elect President Nixon.

"You all killed him." She pointed her finger at me. "And they're going to kill you, too, Billy. Send you to Vietnam so they can watch football."

She grabbed her coat and hat from the hallway and returned to face the adults. "I cannot live with murderers. I am leaving you forever. Forever, I say."

With a dramatic flourish, she opened the front door and departed. Frigid air swept in and battled the cigarette smoke for air superiority.

"Bye, sis."

The adults returned their attention to the television. Someone chuckled. Someone else muttered that Stevie would be fine.

Honestly, my sister went through this sort of drama with us at least once a month, it seemed. She'd walk five houses down the street and spend a night or two at her friend's house, where she would breathe smoke-free air and eat proper food for dinner.

"Hey, Billy." One of my uncles. "Get me another beer, will you, kid?"

"Make that two, please."

"Three, please."

Very polite, my family.

Noting the absence of anything in the kitchen resembling a Christmas dinner, I decided to visit my own refuge, the house of Brian Lincoln, my best friend. Bundling up with coat, knit cap, and gloves, I headed out into the barren wastes of Xenith, Ohio.

* * *

Dead calm and gray skies greeted me outside. Frozen grass crunched beneath my gym shoes as I cut across the lawns of our post-war, brick, matchbox-sized cookie-cutter neighborhoods. Nothing stirred. Not even the dogs.

No children played outside. Playing inside with their presents, no doubt. My present that year? Dad rewired my desk lamp.

The stinging cold provided incentive to move with haste, and I covered the three blocks to Brian's house without incident. Upon approaching their front door, it occurred to me that a telephone call to warn them might have been wiser, but oh well.

Brian opened the front door and the storm door, and stood looking at me as if I had arrived from some distant country. "Hi, Bill."

"Hi, Brian."

We stood looking at each other.

His mom shouted from within the house. "Let him in, Brian. For God's sake."

Brian pushed the storm door further open, and I entered the Lincoln house.

Warmth.

My friend closed the front door behind us and pushed a rolled-up rug across the bottom. "You should have called."

"Sorry." A shrug.

Their living room was like ours, but without beer cans, ashtrays, and uncles. No one sat on the couch or the easy chair, and though none of it was new, all of it was tidy and clean.

His mom, in her apron, bustled into the room with her trademark smile and concerned frown all wrapped into one. "Merry Christmas, Billy." She placed her oven-warm hands on my frozen face and pressed. "Your cheeks are like icebergs. Stand on the heat register. Would you like some hot chocolate?"

Would I like some hot chocolate? "Yes, ma'am."

Soon after, Mr. Lincoln, in his worn winter jacket, came up the stairs from the basement with one of his many toolboxes. In that basement workshop of his was, to my young mind, every tool ever conceived by humanity. It was a wonderland. Things with dials. Things with levers. Things to pound other things, or twist them, or rip them.

My dad's workbench had a hammer, some pliers, a few screwdrivers, and a roll of electrical tape.

Mr. Lincoln glanced at me, with my steaming cup grasped between my hands, and nodded. "Merry Christmas, Billy."

"Merry Christmas, sir."

With a shout, Mrs. Lincoln stopped him and put a bag of something that smelled good in his free hand. “Wish them Merry Christmas. Be back by dinner.”

As his father departed, Brian looked at me. “We could go downstairs and watch TV.”

His mother corrected him. “Or, now that Billy has thawed out, you two can go take a walk and get out of my hair while I cook.”

She replaced my threadbare hat and gloves with thicker ones that used to belong to her husband, as well as a scarf. They were all too large for me, but they were warm.

We looked like polar explorers now, and thus equipped, we stepped out through the hatch onto the frozen surface of Mars.

“Am I allowed to stay for Christmas dinner?”

Brian shrugged. “I guess.”

We set off for Mars Station Zebra. Brian’s street ended with a stretch of recent concrete. Beyond that lay frozen desolation.

We scrambled to the summit of a nearby jumbled hill of dirt and torn tree trunks, which provided a vantage point to survey the best route of advance.

“There’s been no communications with Zebra for seventy-two Martian hours.” Brian raised his hand to shield his eyes from the non-existent glare. “There, on the other side of that vast desert.”

“Those poor souls. Tilling this feeble arid soil.”

“Indeed.”

A quarter mile away, just inside the far tree line, a small hunting cabin we had visited many times, which now bore the name of the ill-fated Mars settlement, waited for us.

Frozen heaps of red and orange soil stretched out before us as we pressed ahead through the bitterly cold air. Avoiding pools of frozen methane, we made the best time possible as our sneakers crunched the icy ground.

I checked my wrist monitor for system vitals. “Oxygen usage normal.”

Our scarves seemed plausible ventilators.

Brian’s muffled walkie-talkie voice confirmed the grim possibilities of our rescue mission. “We’ll need our oxygen reserves for any survivors.”

In the distance, the dark, menacing mountains of Mars loomed with foreboding, their peaks dusted with carbon dioxide snow. Sharp, jagged objects in the tortured ground threatened to pierce our atmospheric suits.

We paused as we neared the tree line. I raised my gloved hand to my ear. “Earth Central, this is Space-Captain Wehman and Space-Captain Lincoln. Do you read, over?”

Only the Martian wind replied.

Brian slapped his hands together. “We’re on our own.”

Mars Station Zebra sat nestled near the head of a small wooded draw. We cautiously approached using only hand-signals. The wood creaked as I stepped onto the porch.

“Check for survivors,” Brian said.

With a nod, I was inside the old cabin. Beer cans. Liquor bottles. Empty bags of chips.

And a little girl.

Brian followed me in, and spotting her, he came to an abrupt halt. “Debby?”

Wrapped in a fur coat far too large for her, she huddled in the cabin’s corner. Her brown eyes stared back at us, and dark hair peeked out from under her knit cap.

My friend stepped forward and knelt beside the five-year-old. “What are you doing out here?”

“Hi, Brian.”

I put my hand to my ear. “Earth Central, we have located a survivor. Please advise.”

Brian gave me a quick look – an incredulous look – and scooped Debby up in his arms. “Let’s go, Star-Captain.”

* * *

Halfway back across the frigid Martian desert, Brian, breathing heavily, handed the fur coat-ensconced urchin to me. “Your turn.” She wrapped her arms around my neck.

Her voice in my ear was low and trembled. “You’re my hero, Star-Captain.”

Before or since, no one has ever called me their hero.

When we arrived at the Lincoln house, Brian’s mom set to work. She tsked and tutted as she wrapped the child in a blanket and set her at the kitchen table with a mug of hot chocolate.

"Sweetie, why were you out at that old cabin? It's so cold today."

"Daddy's busy. Said stay away."

Mrs. Lincoln frowned. "He probably meant to stay quiet, not go freeze to death." She patted Debby on top of the head. "Next time, come visit us instead, okay?"

"Yes, ma'am." The little girl smiled.

"Brian, go down the street and see if Debby's father is home."

While we waited for Brian to return, I kept Debby company in the kitchen and sipped at another cup of hot, steaming love. In the hallway, Brian's mom was tsking and tutting over the fur coat as she plucked pieces of dead leaves out of it.

"Such a shame. Debby, you mustn't take your mother's coat out of the house. You want it to stay nice for when you're grown up."

"Yes, ma'am." Debby put her hand on my hand and looked up at me. "Are you an orphan, too?"

My eyes widened in response.

Mrs. Lincoln shook her head. "Sweetie, you aren't an orphan. You still have your daddy. An orphan loses their daddy *and* their mommy."

Brian returned and announced that there was no car in Debby's driveway.

"Set a place for Debby at the dining table, Brian." A moment later, his mom spoke again. "And one for Billy." She looked at me. "You're staying for Christmas dinner, right?"

Am I staying for Christmas dinner? "Yes, ma'am."

Debby's soft little hand still clutched mine. "You *are* just like me."

Brian's mom made me call home for permission. At a mere eleven years of age, holding the switch hook to fake a call was not new to me.

"Mom says Merry Christmas to you."

This drew a smile from Mrs. Lincoln.

I have no idea whether she believed my ruse or if I had provided plausible deniability. It was not worth rumination. I took my seat.

The Lincoln Family was not rich, but that evening I dined like a king. Brian and his older sister sat across from Debby and me, respectively. Mr. and Mrs. Lincoln reigned over us from each end. With heads bowed, we thanked the Almighty One, and afterwards Debby and I exchanged looks and smiles that spoke to our mutual good fortune.

* * *

After dinner, after dessert, we put on our warm things to escort Debby back to her home. That prospect brought a quietness to the little girl, but she said nothing. Mrs. Lincoln put the fur coat in a cardboard box and handed it to Brian.

"Wish Mr. Dirne a Merry Christmas."

With a nod, we were outside, and in a matter of minutes, we reached their house and rang the bell.

And rang it again.

Getting cold, I reached out to ring a third time just as the door opened.

Debby's father stood on the other side of the glass storm door in his underwear.

We looked at him. He looked at us and his daughter, and opened the door.

"Come on in, boys."

I assumed he meant Debby, too, and pushed her in front of me as we entered the warmth of the little living room that mirrored all the living rooms on our streets.

"Have a seat, boys." He closed the front door and staggered off to the kitchen. Debby climbed onto the couch and took a spot between Brian and me. My eyes widened when her father returned with three opened bottles of King of Xenith beer. Without ceremony, he gave Brian and me cold bottles and clinked his own against them. "Merry Christmas, boys."

My official first drink. I'm not particularly proud of that, but there you have it. In retrospect, perhaps not such a good decision. First of many.

After sitting uncomfortably for a spell, it was time to leave. Debby hugged Brian first, and he gave her a quick pat. Debby hugged me with a fierceness that surprised and embarrassed me. When she pulled away, there was moistness around her eyes.

"Thank you for saving me. Goodbye, Star-Captain."

Brian smirked at the carpet.

Debby's father chuckled. "Looks like Deb's taken a liking to you." He smoothed her hair. "Go brush your teeth. Get ready for bed."

Out in the cold, there was nothing more to say other than see you later.

Standing there, cold as I was, it suited me to watch my friend walk the ten houses back to his own home and go inside. Without any great ambition to go towards my own house, I turned to face Debby's. A lone light shone in the front window of an otherwise dark house.

A true star-captain would've burst through that door and borne her away to safety. I knew that. I knew that even then.

* * *

I expected a stern lecture at home, but only snoring greeted me. Poking my head into the living room, I counted six uncles, two aunts, my mom, and my dad arrayed as I had left them, but now all asleep. More cans and bottles and ashtrays. No evidence of Christmas Dinner.

Upstairs, my sister's room, next to mine, was dark. As it turned out, sis was right. Cousin Stevie *was* dead. We wouldn't know that for a long while. The Air Force carried him as missing in action for several years until the Vietnamese discovered and returned his remains. No one saved him, either.

In my room, I threw my new hat and gloves on the bed and hung my coat across the back of my chair. With a sigh, I sat down. The first page of "The Heroic Adventures of Star-Captain Bill Wehman on Mars" waited.

My desk lamp, however, provided no light. I tried the switch again, and again, and... gave up. *Of course.*

Sudden resolution came to me. My hand reached out to grasp that sheet of paper and tore it from my spiral notebook. The waste basket seemed a more appropriate place for it.

SCOTT MACMANN

Gracie

Clear of clouds and vapor trails, the September sky stretched up into the blue. Tom sighed and let go of the bedroom window curtain. *What a beautiful day.*

In the kitchen, his wife Mandy sat at the table with a cup of coffee and her laptop.

"Good morning," he said. "Does Gracie need her fluids?"

Her fingers paused, but she did not look up at him. "Are you serious? Why would you do that to her today? Are you heartless, or just stupid?" Her eyes reflected the glowing screen.

Tom stood there a moment, turned, and left the room. Gracie was curled up on the heat register in the nursery. He bent down and scritched her ears.

Their first Christmas Eve together, Tom and Mandy had been hanging the wreath on their apartment door when a little, gray fluff ball skittered inside.

"A kitten!" Mandy scooped her up.

"No cats!"

"Of course not. We'll put up signs. Put ads in the paper. Poor little kitty." She had nuzzled the purring kitten as Tom frowned at them.

Fifteen years later, that kitten's kidneys were failing.

As a teenager, Mandy had been a vet's assistant, so now she gave Gracie the subcutaneous fluids. A year ago, they had been once a week, but now were the daily ordeal that kept Gracie alive.

He stroked her head. "Mommy says you don't need your fluids today, sweetie." Tears came to his eyes, but he blinked them away. "It's going to be all right."

Tom returned to the kitchen. "What time do we need to be there?"

Mandy did not look up. "I told you once. You obviously didn't care, or else you would remember."

He stared at her. *Why must she snipe at me? Ten? Eleven? Soon.* "I'll get the cat carrier from the basement."

Mandy said nothing.

They kept a mauve cat carrier on the gray metal shelf under the basement stairs. In the dim light, he stared into the dark, dusty cage. A vision flashed from when he was seven years of age. He saw his family's Siamese cat, and Alex's dull, sad eyes looking out at him from within.

* * *

One Autumn day after school, Tom found Alex hanging by the neck from the spare clothesline in the backyard. *The damn neighbor kids!*

In terror, he held Alex up to take the weight off the rope, and through tears, he screamed for his mom.

Precious minutes passed. Screaming for mom. Crying. Kissing his poor Alex.

Then his mother came outside and, seeing him, she snuffed her cigarette on the concrete porch. Her dour expression remained steady as she walked across the grass to him. She untied the knot and took Alex's limp body from him. "Get the cat carrier. He's not dead."

She put him inside and closed the cage door. Those eyes. Soft, sweet Alex slept under the covers with him every night. His best friend's dull stare through the metal bars. *Don't die.*

"Stop crying," she said. "It's going to be all right."

And then one last look. Mom and Alex were gone.

Tom went to his room upstairs. *She said it's all right. Oh, please.* He had wanted to call his dad, but he knew his mom would be angry if he did. He wasn't allowed to talk to him.

He sat at his desk and watched the afternoon light fade into night. He wrapped himself in his arms, bent his head down to the desktop, and sobbed.

It was dark when he heard his mom return. The car turned off. The car door thumped. The front door opened and closed.

He held his breath. *Alex?* Downstairs was silent. He waited. Maybe he should go talk to her? But what if? No. He waited. And waited. At length, he crawled into his cold bed and, in the darkness, missed the warmth of his friend.

The next morning, his mom had already left for work when he came downstairs. On the kitchen table, she had left his lunch money and a packet of instant oatmeal for breakfast.

He never asked about Alex. His mom never told him what happened at the vet.

* * *

Tom blinked. He hadn't thought of Alex in years. That damn neighborhood. He pulled the carrier down off the shelf and headed upstairs.

Mandy and her laptop were not at the kitchen table. He went to the nursery, but Gracie was not where he had left her. The crib and changing table were both piled high with books and papers.

In the living room, the front door was ajar. When he opened it, he saw that Mandy and Gracie were sitting in a sunny spot on the grass. The laptop was on Mandy's lap.

Mandy had pulled up some grass and put it in front of Gracie, who had perked up a bit.

Tom smiled. *Oh, Gracie, you love the dumb grass. For fifteen years, you've been trying to get outside to roll in the grass, and I've been bringing you right back in. Now that you're allowed to be out here, it's too late for you to enjoy.* He stopped smiling.

Tom sat down across from Mandy with Gracie in between them. He scritched her head. Mandy reached out and soothed her fur.

Their hands were so close to touching. *I wish I could put my hand on yours.* Fifteen years hadn't felt like a long time to him. It was the blink of an eye from a better time. His mind wandered.

* * *

Ten years previous. Sitting in the doctor's office. "You are both young and healthy. Try again. Miscarriages happen all the time."

Blink. Stare at the floor. *Do they? Why? How would I know? What's normal? How can this be normal? Not normal for us. What do I say? Thank you?*

Should I look at Mandy? Will she be angry? I love you, Mandy. I do. Will you still love me? I wish I had died instead of our baby. Like Alex died. Would you love me then? He had said nothing.

They stopped to fill the prescription. *Take some drugs. Make the pain go away. Fill the space. Make another baby. This is normal. Get over it.*

He took Mandy home. They said nothing in the car. They said nothing in the house. Mandy went to their room. He stood in the living room and looked at their empty house full of their things. He wandered to the nursery. All ready. He touched the edge of the crib. Their baby would have slept here.

The house was silent.

He went to their bedroom. Mandy was under the covers, staring at the far wall. Gracie had curled up in her arms.

"I'm going into work for a little bit," he said.

I should have said I love you. I should have said we can get through this together. If only the words could come out.

* * *

The clicking of her laptop keyboard intruded.

"For God's sake," he snapped. "Can't you take your nose out of that damn laptop for five minutes?"

Mandy looked at him with dull, sad eyes. She closed the laptop and put it in her shoulder bag. She stood up and walked away towards the driveway.

Tom's mouth fell open.

Her car started. Mandy drove past them out to the street, and she was gone.

Tom looked after her, then at Gracie. A word formed, but stopped. A sudden wave of dread swept across him. *Steady. Be steady.*

He reached out and scritched Gracie's head again. *Poor little kitty.* He opened the door of the cat carrier.

His eyes stung, and his voice quivered. "It's going to be all right, Gracie."

JOHN PICARD

The People's Choice

It had to be explained to him that he would be guarding the most famous body qua body on the planet, three consecutive tours of duty leaving him with little time for recreation, though the name Heather Ganges did ring a dull bell.

"She has her own reality show?" prompted Ms. Copley, the assignment director. "She made a sex tape?"

Lionel, six foot three, two hundred and forty pounds, with a size sixteen neck, and massive – if trembling – hands, shook his head.

"They're saying another one might surface. This time with T-Fat."

"T-Fat?"

"The rapper. My, you have been out of touch."

After leaving active service, Lionel attempted to find work in the financial sector, but got nowhere with only a high school education. While contemplating community college, he signed on with Celebrity Bodyguard Services, one of the few concerns actively recruiting veterans.

"Anyway," Ms. Copley said, "she's more popular than ever, which is why they're beefing up security." She squinted at her computer screen. "According to this, you were awarded a Purple Heart."

"Yes, ma'am."

"*And* a Bronze Star. Very impressive. It also says you received a medical discharge. May I inquire as to the reason or reasons?"

"Allergies."

"Allergies?"

"Yes, ma'am."

"Well. Thank you for your service. Our country depends on heroes

---

* *John Picard is a native of Washington, D.C., currently living in Greensboro, North Carolina. A collection of his stories, Little Lives, was published by Main Street Rag.*

like you to keep us free." Ms. Copley stood. "We're proud to have you aboard at CBS." She thrust out her hand.

Lionel flinched. "Thank you," he said and braced himself for human contact.

* * *

On Lionel's first day on the job, he and Pete, a former Green Beret and his de facto mentor, followed Heather Ganges's Lamborghini Aventador to Stir Crazy on Sunset. They exited the black van and trailed Heather and her two girlfriends to the counter, where they were served by a middle-aged barista with a top knot. The bodyguards retreated to a discreet distance while the women huddled over skinny lattes at a corner table.

"Watch this," Pete said.

In minutes, the coffee shop was swarming with people desperate for a look at the reality star. They took pictures with their phones, called friends, chattered excitedly, or just stared. Lionel and Pete came over and stood at parade rest on either side of Heather's table, prepared to thwart any possible intrusion.

"Thanks, guys," she said in her high-pitched voice. Her face had an exotic, faintly Asian look. Her thick strawberry-blonde hair was tied in a ponytail. Her beige leather mini-skirt was halfway up her tanned thighs.

"You're new," she said to Lionel, looking at him with her dark almond-shaped eyes.

"Yes, ma'am."

"I'm not a ma'am. I'm a Heather."

"Yes, ma– Heather."

More gawkers were squeezing into the shop when someone tripped in the doorway. Stylish women holding shopping bags fell like dominoes. The barista's threats to call the police went unheeded, or, considering the din, unheard.

Lionel's heart began to race. He shifted his weight to his prosthetic knee. "Is it always like this?" he asked.

Pete gave him a look. "Where've you been?"

"Afghanistan, Helmand Province."

For Lionel, the room's clamoring voices suddenly became the cries of screaming hajis. The coffee machine sounded like the rat-tat-tat of Kalashnikovs. Brewing coffee smelled like freshly spilled blood. Dreaming about Lashkar Gah was one thing; reliving it another. The therapist he'd seen before his discharge warned him about flashbacks. He tried to ground himself in the present, as she'd recommended. He clenched his fists. He bit down hard on his lower lip. He talked to the fear, another of her suggestions. He was the biggest, strongest human in the place. What were a bunch of crazed onlookers compared to armed-to-the-teeth Taliban fighters?

Pete leaned over the table. "You might want to think about moving on, Heather."

She raised a finger but otherwise failed to heed Pete's warning. The crowd swelled.

Sweat was trickling down Lionel's sides.

At last, Heather consented to depart the premises. The bodyguards ran interference, clearing a way through the crowd. Lionel, meanwhile, was beating down the panic. Heather exited the coffee shop unscathed as the flashback receded.

* * *

Heather Ganges was forever in the public eye, a strategy to promote her so-called brand. Everywhere she went, paparazzi pursued her, and fans swooned over her. Lionel found himself in places he couldn't even have imagined before: the fanciest restaurants, the poshest boutiques, the swankiest bars, among other trendy hotspots. He sat behind Heather at a fashion show put on by some clothes designer, Donny Bucciarelli. Tall skeletal women paraded back and forth in skimpy dresses and stilt-like heels. He attended his first NBA game, Heather being a huge Lakers fan. With Heather Ganges as a frequent guest on late-night talk shows, he rubbed shoulders with the biggest newsmakers and movie stars of the day.

Still adjusting to life stateside, Lionel spent most of his free time in his sparsely furnished studio apartment. He had no friends or acquaintances to speak of. The ones he had before he enlisted didn't understand him, and he didn't understand them and their petty concerns: thin-crust versus deep-dish pizza, Netflix, the latest app, fantasy football. A history buff before he enlisted, he couldn't read for more than five minutes without losing his place. While he waited for his concentration to return, he watched hour after hour of cable television. One evening, drinking the first of nine beers – the number most likely to stave off nightmares as well as ease his chronic joint and back pain – he caught an episode of *Going, Going Ganges* on TBS.

Heather and her brother Trevor drive to Nordstrom for a shopping spree on the advice of a grief counselor who suggested it as a way to deal with the passing of Heather's cat. The camera follows her and her flaky brother from floor to floor. The highlight of the show is Heather buying a matching skirt and blouse, an obvious ploy to show off her body. The camera follows her into the changing room, where it catches her in various stages of undress. Lionel didn't care for her figure: narrow shoulders, tiny waist, slim hips. Yet Heather Ganges couldn't go anywhere without people eager to be near her, which raised the question of how he could take seriously the protection of a woman who let cameras film her doing the most private things (next week's show was about Heather's monthly bikini wax). Wasn't the job an insult to the men he'd served with?

He passed out at 2 a.m. Despite the beers, he's back in Lashkar Gah: screaming hajis storming the bunker of his already decimated platoon; the air reeking of blood and smoke and sweat; Kalashnikovs deafening in that small space; Cashman taking a bullet between the eyes, Stingly two in the stomach, Dibacco one in the neck. All gone. Lionel, badly wounded, his weapon just out of reach, lunges for it but falls short. The hajis shriek over and over one of the few phrases he knew in their language, which translated to "No prisoners! No prisoners!" Lionel jackknifed off the sofa, his heart slamming in his chest, his underwear soaked through.

As always, the nightmare left him feeling guilty (*Why me? Why was I spared?*) and ashamed (*How could I have lost my whole fucking platoon?*). So he was not in the best mood when he and Pete drove Heather to Smooth Cheeks in West Hollywood for her Brazilian honey waxing. He escaped having to witness the actual procedure, while Pete didn't understand why the camera crew was allowed in, and they weren't.

"Anything wrong?" Heather asked Lionel, who'd not spoken since they parted from the camera crew and entered the van – Lionel and Pete in back, Heather up front with the driver.

"No, ma'am," Lionel said.

"Heather," she said.

"Heather."

She let her chin rest on the back of the seat, then put out her arm. Lionel twisted away, his shoulder banging the door frame.

"He's a little uptight, this guy," Pete said.

"I was just trying to get that string," Heather explained.

Lionel brushed the white thread off his black T-shirt, embarrassed by this show of weakness.

"You're a vet, right?" Heather asked. "A friend of my brother's was in Iraq."

"He won't talk about it," Pete said. "He's one of those hard cases. Aren't you, El?"

Heather said, "Some of my biggest fans are vets. I visit VA hospitals every chance I get. Thank you for your service."

Lionel could just imagine what these hardened veterans thought of Heather Ganges, of the hairless coochie.

As if reading his mind, Heather said, "You don't approve of me, do you? You don't like what I do."

Caught off guard, Lionel stammered, "I... I..."

Heather's plush lips curled into a cryptic smile.

"You'll have to excuse my friend," Pete said. "One too many tours of duty. He thinks you're the bomb, don't you, El." To Lionel, he whispered, "Mook."

She was right, of course. He didn't approve. He didn't approve of what had become of his country. He was appalled by the vulgarity and the trashiness on TV: the four-letter words, the explicit sex talk, the bare skin. Everything was shown, nothing was hidden. All the mystery was being taken out of love and sex. On his walks around South L.A., he was disgusted by the young women he passed with their skin-tight leggings. Everywhere he went, he saw people staring at their cellphones, blind to the world around them, too busy with their twittering and their texting to care about their countrymen fighting and dying eight thousand miles away. And don't get him started about reality shows. What was real about them? *He'd* show them reality.

* * *

"Did you hear?" Pete said. "Heather was nominated by the People's Choice Awards for Best Reality Star."

"They have awards for that?"

"They have awards for everything. It's her first nomination for best all-round, and she's stoked."

"Do we have to be there?"

"Are you joking? Of course we have to be there."

"Can Stan fill in for me?" Stan was the backup bodyguard.

"No way. This is too important. She'll want the first team there on her big night."

"Her big night?"

"Biggest of her career."

"What career?"

"All you do is throw her shade. You need to show a little respect. You need to chill, bro. I mean it."

* * *

He'd had an active sex life before his final tour of duty. It was time, he decided, to get back on that horse. Unfortunately, he hadn't met any ladies since leaving the military, and he was too proud to ask Pete to set him up. He'd never gone to a prostitute or any other kind of sex worker, but he was lonely, and he could really use some feminine company. He searched various online escort services before arriving at the website of one Delilah St. Clair.

They arranged to meet in the lobby of a Holiday Inn Express.

"You're military, right?" she said, sitting on the queen bed and removing her top. She could have been prettier, but she had the kind of body he liked – full breasts, long legs.

"Ex-military," he said. "How'd you know?"

"You scream it, baby. Come here, soldier. That's an order."

He didn't move.

"What's wrong?" Delilah St. Clair said. "Don't you like me?"

He stepped tentatively toward the bed.

"You're shy," she noted. "That's sweet." As he moved closer, he could feel his skin heating up. When she touched his arm, a jolt like an electric current shot through his body. He pushed her away.

"Hey!"

"Sorry," he said. "Sorry," and fled.

* * *

The People's Choice nomination increased the frenzy that was Heather Ganges's life; more berserk fans, more pushy paparazzi. As often as he'd witnessed it, Lionel continued to be dismayed by the reaction Heather evoked from otherwise sane people, their faces full of awe and wonder and sometimes what appeared to be an actual glow, as if reflecting the reality star's near-blinding presence. More and more often, he and Pete acted as a wedge to get Heather from one public place to another through heaving, boisterous crowds.

One Saturday, they were forging a path for Heather and Trevor as they exited WeHo Bistro. Lionel had been up since three, afraid to fall back asleep. Being sleep-deprived made him more vulnerable to flashbacks, but flashbacks made him more reluctant to doze off. Last night, he'd dreamed Cashman was shuffling toward him, his face covered with gore and his eyes popping with anger and blame. Lionel took off running as fast as his dream legs would carry him. Cashman, so plodding in life, was right behind him, matching him step for step. Joining the pursuit was Stingly, holding his intestines inside his body with one hand and shaking a fist at Lionel with the other. Dibacco brought up the rear, fleet of foot despite a gushing carotid artery, shouting curses. Now, as he and Pete were escorting Heather and Trevor to the Lamborghini, the ecstatic faces in front of him turned into haji faces, the squealing voices into haji voices. An arm shot out of the crowd. Lionel grabbed the wrist and gave it a violent twist, a maneuver he'd learned in basic. The fan didn't feel the pain at first, momentarily numbed by the anesthetizing presence of Heather Ganges. But that only lasted a second or two. A video of the incident went viral.

Pete told Lionel he might want to start looking for another job. This was bad, one of Heather Ganges's bodyguards almost breaking a fan's arm. That night, Pete called and asked Lionel to meet him for drinks.

"Good news," Pete said after they ordered beers. "Heather's going to the game on Tuesday, and she wants us both there."

"I'm not fired?"

"You owe me, El. You'd probably be gone if I hadn't told her about your Bronze Star. I think she likes you because you're a survivor." Pete pointed a finger at him. "But what happened yesterday can't happen again."

Lionel sipped his beer.

"What's going on in that thick skull of yours, anyway?" Pete reached across the table as if to touch Lionel's head.

He batted Pete's hand away.

"You're one uptight motherfucker, you know that?"

Lionel took another sip of beer.

"You went through some serious shit over there, didn't you? Have you talked to anyone about it?"

Lionel didn't answer.

"You're not helping yourself by keeping that shit bottled up, you know. What about medication? You on anything?"

"Just this," Lionel said, raising his long neck.

"Tough guy. Don't need nobody or nothin,' right?"

Putting the bottle down, Lionel dropped his shaky hands under the table.

Pete said, "Can't sleep. Can't think straight. Can't get it up. Sound familiar? You got it, bro. Half the men I served with got it."

Lionel stood. "I have to be somewhere." He threw down a ten.

"Tough guy," Pete said.

* * *

Heather and Binge – the tatted-up rock star who was Heather's on-again off-again boyfriend and a semi-regular on *Going Going Ganges* – plus her brother and four of her girlfriends were given front-row center-court seats at the Staples Center for the Lakers versus the Knicks. Lionel and Pete sat at either end of the large group. When Heather was shown on the Jumbotron, there was wild applause but also a smattering of boos, a reminder to Lionel that some people felt the same way he did. The capacity crowd got louder as the game went on. He scanned the rambunctious crowd for assurances that what sounded like high-decibel haji war cries were ordinary Americans enjoying a sporting event.

"Don't you like basketball?" Heather asked him during a time-out. "You don't seem that into the game."

"I'm into it," he said.

"Oh yeah? Who's winning?"

Lionel did a quick check of the scoreboard. "Lakers."

With only minutes left in the final period, Lionel was glancing over his shoulder when he heard a collective gasp. Turning back to the court, he found himself looking at a basketball headed straight for his nose. Heather's manicured fingers swept across Lionel's vision and batted the ball away.

When the moment was replayed in slow motion on the Jumbotron, Heather Ganges received cheers from all eighteen thousand one hundred paying customers. It was all Lionel could do not to bolt in shame.

After they got Heather and her crew safely home, Pete drove Lionel to his apartment. As he was leaving the van, Pete said, "See you at eighteen hundred hours."

"What?"

"The People's Choice Awards, remember?"

"That's tomorrow?"

"And you better bring your game face. I don't mean the one that almost got creamed."

That night, Lionel drank straight from a bottle of Jack as he surfed porn site after porn site. Succumbing to smut always made him feel crummy afterwards. It was a point of pride with him that he'd never watched Heather Ganges's sex tape. But if he couldn't do it, he could look at it. As sometimes happened, a live model who'd linked herself to a video appeared on his computer screen. Tonight, it was a perky blonde rolling around on pink sheets in only heels and panties. These real-time women were more exciting than any video – ideal for getting off. He was almost there when he heard a high-pitched voice say, "Do you know I can see you?"

He stopped. "What?" The voice was coming from the computer.

"I can see you." The blonde, who had Heather Ganges's long eyes and full lips, was peering at him through the camera of his PC, which he hadn't realized until now was two-way. Lionel dropped to the carpet and wrapped his arms around his head.

"Where'd you go, honey?"

Lashkar Gah. He's face down on the bunker floor, dust in his mouth and eyes, the smell of blood in his nostrils. The twisted bodies of Stingly, Cashman, and Dibacco lay around him. Seeing him there, bleeding out, the hajis charge across the bunker, Kalashnikovs raised above their heads.

"I know you're there, honey. I can hear you breathing."

"No prisoners! No prisoners!"

A rifle butt strikes his spine. A boot crushes his knee. He's spat on, beaten, left for dead.

He woke at dawn on the bedroom floor, a carpet burn on his left cheek, his head throbbing. He made coffee. He had to hold the mug with both hands to keep it from spilling. He fixed himself some cereal. He threw it up in the shower.

Later on, Pete fetched him in the van, and they drove to Heather's mansion on Rodeo Drive. They followed the limo she'd hired for the occasion. Lionel took surreptitious sips from his flask and ground the fingernails of his right hand into his palm to stay present. The hallucination was pulsing just below consciousness, restive, wanting back. The limo pulled up in front of the Microsoft Theater. Wearing six-inch heels, Heather stepped out in her Bucciarelli gown – crotch-high slit, lots of sideboob. Lionel and Pete positioned themselves on either side of Heather as she moved toward the red carpet. Barriers of yellow tape restrained the fans and the media.

"They really love you," Pete told Heather, who beamed.

Lionel squeezed his fist tighter. "Be right back," he told Pete and, crouching behind the van, drank copiously from the flask. When he came back, Heather was posing on the red carpet.

"You all right?" Pete asked.

"I'm fine."

"Well, you look like shit. Did you forget to shave, or is that some sort of fashion statement?"

Lionel touched his bristly cheek.

Pete sniffed. "You've been drinking."

"Back off."

"Are you fucking kidding me? What's wrong with you, bro?"

A room inside the Microsoft Theater with stadium seating and a closed-circuit TV had been made available to the bodyguards. Every reality star had at least two. Whenever a winner was announced – Best Intervention, Best Kept Secret, Best Confrontation With A Non-Family Member, etc. – two or three very large men would stand up and cheer while the others cursed and otherwise expressed their disappointment. Lionel refused to join in the general idiocy.

"The big one's next," Pete said.

The names of three men and two women were read out by the master of ceremonies.

"And The People's Choice Award for Best Reality Star goes to... Heather Ganges."

Pete leapt up and fist pumped. The other bodyguards came over and offered Pete and Lionel their grudging congratulations.

Pete's phone was ringing – the limo driver informing them that Heather was about to leave the facility.

"Let's bounce," Pete said. "And make sure you say something nice to her."

They found Heather in the main lobby, surrounded by the media, microphones aimed at her broadly grinning face, paparazzi snapping her as she clutched her trophy to her nearly naked bosom. But Lionel's focus was on Heather's squealing fans. They were standing behind the yellow tape, being stretched thinner and thinner the longer they were separated from their idol. Lionel wiped his moist palms on his pants leg. He reached for his flask.

"Congratulations," Pete said to Heather after she escaped the media.

"Thanks, Pete."

Lionel tried to speak, but his throat was bone-dry. They were approaching the exit. The moment Heather stepped out, the crowd erupted: screaming, waving, pushing. The yellow tape snapped. The horde stampeded.

"No prisoners! No prisoners!"

Lionel fell to the pavement and braced for the blows. Instead, he heard his name spoken in a familiar voice. Heather was squatting next to him.

"Flashback," he muttered.

"It's okay," she said and rested her hand on his shoulder. He felt the scorching heat, the surging voltage, but he tolerated it. Heather got down on her knees, then lowered herself onto her side. She was face-to-face with him now, Lionel oblivious to the crowd standing hushed around him. "Turn your head," Heather directed him. "No, the other way. That's it." Placing her hand on the small of his back, she pressed herself against the length of his body, enfolding him, shielding him.

The cameras moved in.

ANTHONY SCHNECK

Flavor Profile

Watermelons (and I realize this sounds ridiculous, maybe even clinically delusional) don't taste like they used to. I remember biting into meaty, crisp, robustly floral red flesh, but now I find a thin, sugary, artificial taste. Every summer between May and September, the difference becomes increasingly pronounced. By the time leaves begin falling you might as well be eating a giant jellybean. No one seems to be aware of this phenomenon, or no one cares, either of which makes sense (if I'm being objective) given the long list of tragedies and crises and atrocities taking precedence in most people's lives.

I can't pinpoint when, exactly, the watermelon issue became a full-blown obsession, but it probably started with the seeds. For years – decades, centuries – watermelons had seeds. Then, within my lifetime, the seeds turned soft and white. A miracle! An heirloom watermelon from a farmer's market became a surprise, a quaint reminder of a more difficult past. Was this really what we'd dealt with all those years? Seeds everywhere, ruining an otherwise pleasurable dining experience?

Once the flavor began to change, I realized the seeds were the first casualties in a war of attrition. Why did this disturb me so much more than any other disturbing trend or event? Even if I preferred some indelible, irrecoverable flavor from my childhood, the fact of its permanent departure meant I had only to decide whether the current version was acceptable. I had to admit that I still managed to enjoy the fruit.

But no. It *wasn't* acceptable. No one had asked or told me about

---

** Anthony Schneck is a writer who lives in Los Angeles. His work has appeared in LA Review of Books, Book XI, and elsewhere. His short play, "Change the Narrative," was a semifinalist for the American Playwriting Foundation's 2023 Picket Plays contest.*

these behind-the-scenes changes, had provided no warning. Hadn't I accepted enough? Hadn't I allowed external forces to dictate the course of my entire life? Hadn't I always complied with barely more than a complaint at the bar?

These kinds of thoughts plagued me more frequently since I lost my job, which I understand is predictable and trite. I didn't want to become some radicalized loner stuck in my room all day, which is what my boyfriend (technically ex) insinuated might happen if I continued down this obsessive road. He was provoking me – he knows I wouldn't resort to such pathetic ends. What I told Gilbert during our last fight was the truth: unemployment gave me freedom, especially considering the way they treated me. Looking down their noses while performing overtly kind small talk. Maybe I didn't have the same degrees or technical expertise as the founders, but I was still a critical employee. Office supplies, day-to-day tasks everyone assumed happened automatically, with no human input. Did any of them wonder how difficult it was to keep track of the mail at an exponentially expanding medical startup? I'm glad it fell apart, though I would've preferred less tragedy. The flagship spinal implant, which had investors so excited and made them utter phrases like "paradigm-shifter" at all-hands meetings, was apparently killing people. Only a minuscule percentage of patients with previously undiagnosed underlying conditions, I should note. But a medical device company can't really afford to kill anyone.

I knew how to float from job to job, could make ends meet, had done it plenty of times, so my sudden change in status arrived like a sputtering wave breaking over my ankles. But when Gilbert expressed his concerns – plus the objective fact of our arguments, my lack of direction – I agreed to push pause, assuming it would give me time to get back on my feet, grow as a person, and check off whatever boxes he deemed necessary to resume the relationship. He did, I should emphasize, say *pause* and not *end*.

With no job and no relationship, I had time for the first time in my life. An opportunity to satisfy myself! Despite my lack of training and expertise, despite my status as a total outsider, I would figure out what was happening with the watermelons – plenty of discoveries had been made by amateurs. Wasn't Darwin one? The prospect seized hold of me, and I felt emboldened with the self-assigned mission. Wasn't this the kind of "self-starter" attitude so many employers say they desire? Surely I was entitled to a bit of fantasy, some self-indulgence. Especially considering the infinite number of times I had muttered obscenities to myself when filling out a spreadsheet or a timecard or a visitor tag or a snack refill order. What about the series of letters to the FDA I proofread – how many ways can you say "small" or "relatively insignificant" when it comes to sudden death?

Answering the watermelon question bore no resemblance to the relentless quotidian maintenance I'd always performed to make ends meet. And I wanted to follow though just to spite Gilbert (I had to tell him, of course), who said I was being ridiculous and had no business getting into this, which probably wasn't an issue at all.

But I knew watermelon flavors were being changed, and I wanted to find out why, and how, and who. And where.

* * *

Barnswell University touted its world-renowned agriculture department that researched both small-scale plant-breeding experiments and genetic engineering projects for huge agrobusinesses. The program's star seemed to be a scientist named Samuel Sarkowsky, whose credits included pest-resistant corn, beta-carotene-rich rice, soft-seeded guava, extended-crisp cucumbers, fettucine-stringed spaghetti squash, and a zucchini that tasted like pumpkin, to name a few. His work with cucurbits made me suspect he was involved with watermelons, or knew someone who was.

Before planning a trip to Barnswell, I sent Dr. Sarkowsky an email in which I claimed to be a journalist writing a feature about him. He responded quickly, wanting to know the name of the outlet I worked for and what its circulation was. Damn. Not much planning had gone into my plan, so I replied that I was technically a freelancer early in my career and the feature was in its infancy, which is why I couldn't tell him the outlet. There was a lot of interest from a particular nationally recognized magazine, I hinted. If they liked the story, it would certainly be widely read. Sarkowsky said he appreciated my industriousness; he could find time to meet the following weekend if I made it to Methony.

I couldn't afford to stay in a motel for even a few days, let alone indefinitely. And think about gas, meals, incidentals. I had just under a thousand dollars in a savings account – why was I saving at all if not to seize this rare chance to send my life careening down a different path? I could make it work. Online I found a cheap room in a house owned by a woman named Amanda M. Red flags abounded (the description offered repeated assurances that she and her two sons would stay well out of any visitor's way), but I didn't have the luxury of avoiding compromise in my room and board. I booked three nights.

On Friday morning I started driving in what was probably a more wrathful mood than advisable after an annoying text exchange with Gilbert. If Amanda M. turned out to be a psychopath, or I got into an accident along the way, or god knows what else, I wanted someone to know where I was going. No response, left on read. Not an exchange, I guess. It seemed impossible that he simply wouldn't care about what happened to me, wouldn't take an interest in my movements, thoughts, ambitions. *You need to move on*, he told me. *Why can't you just find someone else to sleep with? People do it all the time.*

This was an attack on my very existence, my worldview. Hadn't we shared something special, unique? If he was so ready to find a new partner, had he ever cared about me? What's the point of continuing to live if moving on meant apathy, and maintaining hope was pathetic? I texted him as infrequently as I could manage.

Gilbert's steadfast disengagement simmered in my head for the first hour-and-a-half of the drive. Then the subdivisions and shopping centers faded away to reveal expanses of cow pastures punctuated by the gargantuan houses of wealthy equestrians or part-time farmers who bought up the land and were one of the few buffers against developers who wanted to raze it all and replace the green-gold fields with mini malls and more subdivisions. I relaxed, observed the grazing cows and horses in my peripheral vision. Envied them.

Pastures dissolved into the distance, the road narrowed, and deciduous forest rose up on both sides of the pavement just before I got on the interstate and began several hours of mind-numbing progress. When I finally exited the gray-green monotony, I was transported to a halo of idyllic countryside that marked the beginning of the fantasyland surrounding Barnswell.

Amanda lived in a modest rancher, its beige paint cracking around the roof corners, dandelions threatening to overrun the grass lawn, in a neighborhood mostly devoid of students. The sun burned too hot, hung too high for early evening. Unnatural, or the latitude? She opened the door and barely said hello before a series of screams made her whip her head around and shout, "Cut that out!" while I tried to look beyond her frame. Two boys thudded into view, tangled up in each other as they shouted incoherently and fell to the floor. Amanda looked like she would rip them apart, but instead told them to go to their rooms, keep their hands to themselves. They moped off. "That's Ashton and Grayson," she explained before leading me to a room at the end of a narrow hall. "I sleep on the pullout in the living room," she said. "The three of us use the bathroom at the other end of the house. You can use the one across the hall. The kitchen is available, just clean up after yourself. Here's a key to the front door, and one to the room." She picked up a crumpled set of scrubs in the hallway. I thanked her, closed the door, and lay down on the twin bed, ignoring the hunger clawing at my gut.

* * *

Dr. Sarkowsky emailed me the next morning, asking if we could push our 11 AM meeting to later in the afternoon. It gave me time to absorb the campus, try to interpret the energies that made some people believe it possessed mystical powers – something about a unique convergence of the earth's magnetic fields. I couldn't perceive any unusual vibrations, but it did feel instantly cozy, cocoonish. Brick building after brick building, all in a vaguely neoclassical style trying to emulate some ideal form of education as it existed in the early 1800s. My school had been a few office buildings along a highway; I couldn't imagine going to class in columned halls with marble floors. Huge portraits of revered men I didn't know hung in the entrances to all of them. No one questioned my presence, but still I felt treasonous, like I might be exposed and sentenced to death.

I'd been lying on the grass, reading in the style of imagined college students, for more than two hours when I realized it was well after lunch. I broke into a jog toward Weber Hall, my heartrate rising and my anxiety spiking – my backstory was incredibly flimsy. No pen or notepad or recorder, I was showing up by myself to... chat? About an article that may or may not appear in a magazine? This would never work, it was so dumb, so so so dumb. I was an idiot for even attempting it. I just hoped he wouldn't be too harsh, would see straight through my obvious lies and quietly ask me to leave.

"Where's your notebook? Don't writers carry notebooks everywhere?" Dr. Sarkowsky immediately asked after shaking my hand.

I stuttered slightly. "I'd like to have an informal conversation first, just to get a feel for your work and who you are and all that."

This response satisfied him, or he didn't actually care, because he turned away and started talking as he led me from the marbled entrance hall through a series of linoleum-floored corridors. Scientists often operate behind the scenes, he explained. He didn't think people realized how much of an impact they had on everyday life. The public only experienced the end result, never the process, the excruciating amount of time and effort that could go into a failure – which may in fact be an important step on the way to success. This work I'd emailed him about, for example, was something that would change the future of food for the entire world, yet most people wouldn't blink an eye when it finally arrived. He invited me to think about how massive that was: food itself. Transformed. An agricultural revolution all over again, undergirded by the most advanced science in human history.

"As the climate changes," he said, "this work could prove lifesaving, not just lucrative, though ideally it'll be both." He laughed to himself. I added a laugh too. Ask questions, I told myself. Have a conversation, get information, that's what journalists do.

Dr. Sarkowsky turned into his office, a warmly lit room packed densely with sagging bookshelves, two computers, framed degrees, and a handful of pictures – at least one with a politician I recognized. Noticing the direction of my gaze, Sarkowsky said, "I gave some testimony for a bill Senator Bullock spearheaded." He paused, but didn't elaborate. Silence took over the room.

"So," he began, mercifully. "What do you want to know?"

"Yes," I replied after fixating on a dour-looking book called

Polyphenols in Plants. "Well, I'm interested in... I'm looking to get a sense of what you're currently doing. Specifically watermelons, I have some questions about watermelons."

He smiled and folded his hands across his chest as he leaned back in his chair. "What can I tell you about those incredible cucurbits?"

I decided to lay out my theory, my observations, how I'd concluded that watermelon flavors had been altered, and what's more, they'd been altered to taste like artificial watermelon flavor, that is, like watermelon candy. I told him about the samples I'd collected over the months and years, my amateur tests, my subjective flavor evaluations, my results. He listened patiently with a smile threatening to break out from the corners of his mouth.

When I finished, he looked at me with the same near-smile. "What's your question?"

"Um, is it true? Or am I going completely out of my mind?"

He sat up straighter in his chair and stretched his arms. He was more athletic than the graying, spectacled scientist who smiled in his online university bio. "You're absolutely right," he bluntly said. "More or less. Myself and the team here have been working on this project for the past several years, in conjunction with some commercial seed companies I can't mention. But no one has ever asked about specific flavor profiles of the cultivars we've been producing and marketing. Huh. You're the first person – first consumer, just a regular member of the public – to say anything about it at all."

"So... you *are* making watermelons that taste like watermelon candy?"

He laughed, "That's one way to put it. The nuanced truth is more complicated. I'm happy to talk you through whatever you'd like. You know, the work may sound futuristic or dense or super technical to a layman, but on a basic level I'm playing a role that humans have played since the dawn of agriculture. I modify plants to make them more appealing for consumption. What we've found is that while seedless varieties have revolutionized the watermelon market and changed consumer behavior, there's still a ton of work to be done in the arena of optimizing flavor. And nutrition, for that matter, though I happen to believe flavor is the more important first step. If you can create a fruit or vegetable people love to eat, one with high yields and pest resistance and commercial viability and so on, you can go back and tweak the nutrition. In a kind of crude sense, it's analogous to the way parents drown vegetables in ketchup to get a toddler to eat them."

"Aren't watermelons appealing enough as it is?" I asked. "I mean, they're basically nature's version of candy."

"Aha!" he barked, as though he'd set a trap for me. "*Nature's* version of candy. The conditions of nature have changed. Now that we have the ability to deliver concentrated doses of shelf-stable sugar to virtually anyone, anywhere, any time, so-called 'nature' can't compete. How many kids are going to opt for a fresh watermelon over a cheap candy or juice? I'm leveling the playing field. Artificial watermelon flavoring is a paltry attempt to recreate the flavor of actual watermelons, but that says nothing about the quality of the flavor itself. What I asked is: why not reverse the process? People love the artificial version too. Might it be easier to engineer a living watermelon's flavor than to replicate it synthetically? And could this turn out to be more appealing to the majority of the public than the original flavor?"

He pulled his chair close to his desk and looked at one of the computers. "Here," he said, "we've been conducting subjective flavor response surveys for nearly five years now. A couple interesting trends. One: respondents 65 and over are least likely to prefer the most successful of our so-called 'artificially flavored' watermelons – the technical moniker is Tri-869 – but 18 to 24-year-olds prefer it 79% of the time. What's more, even in just the five years that we've been collecting this data, overall preference for the 869 type has gone from 49% to 56%, certainly a statistically significant trend given our data set. Not to be crass, but a preference for the old watermelon taste will literally die out."

He spun the monitor around to show me proof. I stared uncomprehendingly at the reams of numbers and cells, but I said, "Hmmmm, interesting. People like the real watermelons less than the fake ones?"

With a condescending smile, he replied, "They're *all* real watermelons. Picture this scenario. You're a single mother of three kids, all in elementary school. You're struggling to make ends meet, you work two jobs. When you go to the store, it's easy to toss a bag of candy in your cart – the kids will get excited for it, it's a more efficient caloric bang for your buck, and so on. You know it's not the healthiest option, but convenience plus price plus satisfaction makes the choice simple. But what if you could buy actual fruit that would deliver the same level of sweetness and flavor as the piece of candy? And what if your kids knew that too? Wouldn't you be more inclined to buy the fruit? It's healthier, it tastes just as good as the hardened corn syrup that rots your teeth and leads to all kinds of chronic disease, right?"

"Right," I repeated, nodding at the fenced-off numbers on the screen.

"Listen." Dr. Sarkowsky seemed to pull himself out of a dream. "I've got a dinner soon, but why don't you come by the farm tomorrow? It's about 20 minutes away, we have all kinds of cultivars there, I can show you up close how we develop and grow these plants. Not just watermelons. And you haven't said anything about a photographer, but that would be a perfect place, it's really beautiful out there – it's the south side on one of the foothills, incredible views."

"Oh." I shook myself back to life. "Right. Photos we can do later. Sorry, I didn't mention anything about that. This is just the first stage." I tried to affect an authoritative tone.

"Not a problem," he replied while I imagined ways out of the grift. "Just wanted to give you the option. Still, we can continue this conversation."

He handed me a piece of paper with the address, then led me back into the marbled hall. After he disappeared, I stepped into the nascent dusk, where the comforting warmth of Southern air pried open the icy, air-conditioned grip of the office. Everywhere it smelled like freshly cut grass, and a motor moaned in the near distance.

* * *

On the way back to Amanda's, I stopped at a supermarket to pick up snacks that would tide me over until the next day, when I promised myself I'd splurge on a proper meal. Walking through the automatic doors of this unfamiliar grocery store produced an instant sense of calm. A single building satisfying every nutritional need – a sacred space, a modern church, a place where the willing can witness spiritual transformation. Animals sacrificed, cut into their most desirable bits, packaged neatly and organized by species, then body part. Offerings of grain and vegetables, products of the earth laid out on refrigerated racks and stacked on crates. No shame or guilt over the waste the abundance implied.

In the snack aisle, I picked up several packages and flipped them over to read the ingredients, hoping to find one devoid of chemicals. Plain potato chips. I also grabbed a bag of popcorn, then headed to the produce section. Baby carrots, the stripped-down version of ugly carrots not fit for sale. Hummus, chilled. Seedless watermelons were on sale for 29 cents a pound, a cosmic sign. I leaned down, knocked on several, trying to discern ripeness. I wondered what kind they were – you never saw different varieties lined up next to each other, like apples, at the store. Maybe I would take a slice to Sarkowsky for identification. In the stationary aisle I picked out a couple nice-looking pens and what I thought most closely resembled a reporter's notebook. Might as well have them on hand.

I waddled up Amanda's front lawn, attempting to balance my haul from the store. When I offered to split the watermelon, she pursed her lips in a look of disgust. "I'm not a big fan of watermelon," she said. "It's a texture thing. Feels like you're eating styrofoam or something." She shrugged and left the kitchen while I took the chips, carrots, hummus, and popcorn to my room. I texted Gilbert to let him know I made it and to see what he was doing. No response. It was a Friday night, he must be out. With? Where? I crunched on chips and carrots before falling asleep early, sick of consciousness.

* * *

Sarkowsky stood in the parking lot outside a small building resembling a log cabin, set back among hills where the forest was so dense and the roads so winding you couldn't see where you were driving until you'd arrived. He was wearing chino shorts and a collared short-sleeve shirt, making him appear even more athletic and youthful than yesterday. His appearance shook my assumptions again; a scientist with firm calves and toned shoulders suggested a lack of seriousness, though I knew that was unfair. Was I attracted to him? Or jealous? My own arms and legs shot out straight with barely a ripple of muscle on their way to hands and feet. Both? Neither? He smiled as I pulled up.

"Thanks for coming out here," he said. "This is closer to my natural habitat, and I should have more time for you today. It's where most of the new fruit and vegetable cultivars are initially grown before we test them at scale on one of our larger properties. We call this one Baxter. It's 12 acres, has a few different soil types that we carefully regulate on both organic and conventional plots. Kind of ironic that 'conventional' means pesticides, but that's the power of industry for you. They make the whole thing go."

The inside of the building belied its rustic exterior. Screens, glass cases containing seedlings in perfect rows, tubes of soil ranging from reddish-yellow to nearly black, and lamps emitting various colors and intensities of light filled the room. A long hallway ran straight from the front door, with offices grafted onto both sides.

"The cucurbit plots start a hundred meters or so out back," Sarkowsky told me as we walked down the hall.

We exited the building to a view of nearby hills swelling into distant mountains. Amid the chaos of an untouched forest, these 12 acres looked like a little Eden, row after row of fruits and vegetables, beanstalks, cornstalks, vines, bushes, unidentifiable greens poking out of the dirt, marking the location of their buried nutritional treasure.

"Here we are," Sarkowsky said as he stepped off the path and into rows of vines with watermelons in all shades of green, yellow, and orange attached, resting on the ground like unexploded bombs. "We've got more than a hundred cultivars in development at any given moment, but this year there are seven that we've focused on, with these two here the most promising for commercial purposes. One of the companies we work with is particularly interested in this guy–" He pointed to an oblong orb. "–which we're calling Junior, after JR, after Jolly Rancher, which we obviously can't use. It should be easier than it is to reverse-engineer the taste of these things. But none of the flavor producers will give up their proprietary blends, so it does involve some guesswork."

I bent down to touch it. It was just a watermelon. It felt and looked like all the rest I'd seen and felt in my life.

"Disappointed?" Sarkowsky said with a smile.

"No, it's not that, it's just... I don't know what I was expecting."

"There's one inside that we picked a couple days ago. I'll let you try it when we're done out here." Sarkowsky swept his arm over the field, its greens extending into the forest. "For all the science we have," he said, "there's nothing that can touch the immensity of nature's total power."

"So why mess with it in a lab?" I asked. "All this tampering sounds a bit... I don't know, unhealthy?"

He scoffed. "What most anti-GMO crusaders and other radical whackjobs don't appreciate is that even with the advanced techniques we have available to us for optimizing produce, the essential work is largely the same as it's been for thousands of years. These watermelons come from seed, not from a petri dish. Someone still has to grow them. A farmer has to till the soil, plant the seeds, irrigate and fertilize the fields, fight disease and pests. Rent or buy land, equipment, storage facilities. Deliver the product to market, ideally turn a profit. No one can tell me this process isn't natural."

Kneeling down alongside me, he grasped a vine attached to a miniature watermelon. "As you see, this watermelon is just as real as a watermelon from ten or a hundred or five hundred years ago. Of course they're *different*, the same way everything under the sun changes dramatically over time. That's not news. We have to keep growing, improving – otherwise we'll stagnate and get overtaken by weeds. But how can you look at this," he asked while picking the fruit off the ground, "know it sprouted from a seed placed in dirt, then transformed into a juicy, sweet fruit, and *not* be in awe at the power of nature? This *is* natural, there's nothing more natural than growing an edible plant in the earth. We are merely iterating on God's work. And look, the reality is that no single cultivar will ever reach 100% market saturation, or even 90 or 80 or 70, probably.

"One thing to remember," he continued after a pause, "is that the market will decide. I'm most satisfied when we can deliver a product people didn't even know they wanted or preferred. We've opened their senses to a new experience. What's more, we have the ability to measure this shift in experience, we have the data to back it up. Not even half a century ago you got what you got, no real say in the matter except maybe chocolate or vanilla. We don't live in that world anymore."

He stopped again and looked at the mountains. "That's human

ingenuity, that's how we've survived as a species and how we've come to dominate this planet, and it's how we're ultimately going to save it and ourselves. The soil is losing nutrients, people are getting sicker, most currently viable farmland will be flooded or eroded beyond recognition in the next century. We need to think about how we can mitigate these inevitabilities. How do we deliver adequate nutrition to an exploding population on land that literally doesn't make carrots, or kale, or whatever else, like it used to? The financial incentive helps. People can't just keep these innovations to themselves, after all."

He still held the vine in his hand. I didn't know what I thought, really, only that I liked the way watermelons used to taste, and I wanted to call Gilbert to ask what he thought. My heart suddenly dropped in my chest and I wished I hadn't come. This was stupid, pointless, this was for no one, everything I discovered I *would* keep to myself. I opened the notebook and wrote *why am I doing this* over and over again in a pantomime.

"Come on," Sarkowsky said. "I'll let you taste what we have up at the main building."

* * *

"Aha!" He smiled as he pulled two watermelons from the fridge. "They haven't been gobbled up by grad students. Try these – the one on the left is what you might call an old-style fruit, it's seeded. Less appealing, according to our research, than the one on the right, which is one of the Juniors that should reflect what you can call scientifically enhanced flavoring." He glanced at the notebook still in my hand, which I dutifully opened to write *scientifically enhanced flavoring* followed by *??????????*

"When's the last time you had a seeded one?" he asked as he handed me a slice of the first. I couldn't remember. "Just twenty years ago," he went on, "most store-bought watermelons had seeds. Now you almost have to go out of your way to find them. Seedless are still more expensive to produce because you make a double-chromosome watermelon, then cross it with a normal melon. It's called a triploid, and it's not genetically modified, contrary to what you might think."

"So it's like an infertile offspring? Like a liger?"

Sarkowsky laughed. "Well, I guess in a way. Like a liger or a mule or a zonkey."

"It sounds almost cruel, creating these chromosomally screwed-up plants that can't reproduce."

He laughed again. "Well, fortunately they *are* only plants, and more fortunately for us, we can still eat them. It does, however, make the task of breeding newly flavored seedless varieties a bit more complicated than producing seeded cultivars, but at this point there's no denying the advantages of seedless. Extra R&D invariably pays off. In the long run, anyway."

The seeded slice was crisp, cold, an intensely red color. It was sweet, but not overpoweringly so; it had a complex, floral taste with an almost umami-like note that made me want to chew deeper, harder into the flesh. Sarkowsky produced a paper cup. "For the seeds," he explained. "We save those around here."

Then I took the slice of Junior he'd cut. It was closer to pink than red, just as cold and crisp. It tasted much more like candy than any I'd had recently. It hit my taste buds directly with a dose of sugar, and the remainder felt too weak to stand up to the initial saccharine assault. It was good, but not nearly as good as the first slice. I told Sarkowsky.

"But the Junior does taste more like candy, doesn't it?"

I confirmed that it did.

"Depending on where you live," he said, "you might have to get used to it. Once people get a hold of this, there's no going back. Again, the data simply points in that direction, we're following the path laid out for us." I nodded and scratched *following the data* in the notebook.

We walked to the front entrance. "So," he started casually, "what are next steps? I imagine you'll need biographical information from me, still have to do photos, and we didn't really talk all that much about my academic background or experience. I can certainly think of a lot that would be relevant to your article."

"Well, I'll talk to the editors, there's probably a long way to go, as I mentioned." I hastily added. "But this is good, very interesting, very timely, something people would like to read about. Here's my number, I'll keep you updated. If there's anything else you think I should know, give me a call."

He nodded wordlessly. “By the way,” I said as I was getting into my car, “I picked up a watermelon at the store last night. Can you tell me what kind it is?” I opened the back door and hauled out the sliced-open half I’d saved.

Shifting into scientist mode, Sarkowsky narrowed his eyes. “That looks like it could be a Captivation, maybe a Fascination, but to be sure I’d have to take a closer look. They’re pretty similar. Most people wouldn’t even notice a difference.”

* * *

Lying down on the bed in Amanda’s house, I realized I was starving. I waited until the noise of boys wrestling died down, then walked into the living room. Amanda was reading a magazine, the kids were watching TV and eating some kind of packaged cookie.

“Do you know any good places to eat? Something relatively cheap, if possible.”

Amanda dropped the magazine facedown in her lap and sighed. “Everybody loves the Gaslight Tavern, that’s kind of the famous Methony spot. Just don’t go there too late at night unless you wanna deal with a bunch of drunk college kids. They’ve got a burger and beer for ten bucks if you go before 6.”

I thanked her and told her I’d finished my work early, so I’d be leaving that night. She responded that there were no refunds. I said I understood, she worked up a smile and replied, “We really enjoyed having you! You’ll be getting a good review from me.”

The unremarkable burger hung heavily in my stomach as I settled in for a monotonous night drive. I called Gilbert and left him a message, asked him to give me a call back whenever he had a chance, no big deal.

Fifteen minutes later my phone started buzzing. It was Sarkowsky. He realized that sometimes these kinds of stories can demonize science, or make people alarmist about technology, and he hoped to avoid that. He knew the story might not happen, he just wanted to clarify, add a few things he’d thought of after I’d left. He always second-guessed himself, he said, laughing uncomfortably. Maybe it was the scientist’s curse to go over and over things to make sure they’re right.

“What we’re doing isn’t exactly unique,” he said. “We’re at the forefront, of course, we're advancing the science and implementation, but realistically every food you buy at the supermarket is undergoing some kind of similar process. Well, most of them. A certain amount of individual control must be ceded to experts, specialists.

"I'll frame it another way. You have to trust the advances that allow you to achieve this level of comfort. Otherwise we wouldn't live so well. Nothing can stop, let alone reverse, this process. And no one is saying the old stuff has to go into the trash. There are farmers and independent suppliers who will continue to fulfill the desires of a dwindling market, as long as one survives. It may sound harsh, but that's how progress works."

I squinted into the oncoming headlights, the red tail lights, and the blurred sodium glow of the streetlights. I said I understood, then ended the call.

THOMAS WRIGHT

Anglo-Irish

"I'll tell you the story of Tom O'Reilly; shall I begin it? That's all that's in it!"

My uncle put on Ray-Bans to protect his eyes from the rising sun, which showered pound coins on the windscreen of his silver Transit van, and the flat Cambridgeshire countryside around the empty A1. The glasses looked cool against the driver's pale, chiseled features, and set off his designer stubble and slick-backed Superman hair, but clashed a bit, perhaps, with his grubby blue boiler suit.

"The future's so bright;" Uncle Stephen crooned in ersatz American, "I gotta wear shades. My future, that is," he added, in a classless, placeless English accent, "not Tom's. He's pub-crawling towards extinction."

We were hurtling towards Huntingdon, in early June 1988, on the first day of my summer job as a 'skivvy' for my uncle's three-man gang of builders, a week after I'd finished my A-Level exams. The van was fridge-cold, and the smoke from his cigarette kept getting up my nose, but that didn't blunt my excitement about the work (and working-class) experience awaiting me. Neither did Uncle Stephen's unflattering word-sketches of the crew members. He'd dubbed Trevor 'Johnny Bulldog' and dismissed his fellow brickie and co-boss as 'if-I-know-my-place-I'll-always-have-one English'; Tom, the team's 'navvy', wasn't even worth branding or caricaturing apparently.

"Tom's Irish?" I rasped through my passive-smoker's cough, keen to display interest, hungry for info.

"*Stage* Irish."

He squeezed the accelerator: eight-eight, eighty-nine – speed warped

---

* *Born in Cambridgeshire (UK), Thomas Wright has Irish and British citizenship. Since completing his BA in Modern History at Oxford University, he has authored several books, plays, stories, and articles. He currently lives in Genova, Italy.*

enough to satisfy, surely, even a youngish man (he was twenty-seven) who always seemed to be in a hurry. Slipping my left hand under my U2 T-shirt, I clasped my Virgin Mary medal and muttered an Ave Maria. Too scared to look at the road, I gazed out of the passenger window – hedges, fields, and farms, on repeat, blurred into a strip of a sickly green.

"What's 'stage Irish'?"

I sputtered, to take my mind off his harum-scarum driving, and eager for an insider's take on an issue that fascinated me. Like my mother, Uncle Stephen never described himself as Irish, or even Anglo-Irish, though it was hard to imagine him (or anyone) matching his sister's born-again conviction she was a 'purebred Brit, not a Brigid'. Yet their parents had been Irish-born, and speaking, and proud of it. My grandmother – a tiny, wiry, cobalt-eyed country woman from Limerick – had died three years previously. She'd been the great friend of my childhood (my grandfather, meanwhile, had died just after my uncle's birth). Each Sunday, holy day, and every other day, she'd taken me to a cold, whitewashed church full of Irish exiles, immersing me in Catholicism's dotty dogma and sacred showbiz. She'd lavished traditional Irish songs and stories on me and introduced me to Irish poetry, which I'd decided to study at university, from September, as part of my so-called *English* Literature course. I said a rosary to her every night, with the ice-blue beads she'd left me – though I no longer believed in God, or Mary, I still believed in her. I described myself as 'Anglo-Irish' for her sake, and to annoy my renegade mother and 'Queen-and-Country' English father. I despised their bumptious Britishness, wannabe middle-class snobbery, and support for Margaret Thatcher's jingoism, as well as her assaults on the working class. I was sticking my fingers up at them, and all that crap, by working on a building site for my brickie uncle, rather than in a solicitor's office with my father, who'd procured a summer placement for me at his firm without even asking my permission or opinion. "I'm going to be a writer," I'd informed them, spurning the placement, after successfully begging my uncle for a summer job, "and a *bildung* site will be better for my creative development than a solicitor's orifice."

My uncle blew a smoky speech bubble, then filled it with words, spoken in deadpan Bogart mode, but at Ben-Elton breakneck speed.

“Stage Irishness is sham-mock Irishness. ‘To be sure, to be sure’, your grandparents’ dominion-status generation had to put on the Paddy Act when they came over, to offer English bosses and landlords a flattering stereotype. But there’s no sense or justification, in 1988, for Tom turning his life into a rambling Irishman-Englishman joke.”

He recounted a story, to ‘inoculate’ me against Tom’s ‘*Oirish* charm’, about an end-of-building-project party in a ‘ritzy’ hotel, attended by the crew along with various dignitaries and the industry hierarchy, whom my uncle was ‘schmoozing’ in order to secure subcontracts. A wasted Tom had shown my uncle up in front of the ‘bigwigs’, by emerging from the lavvy ‘yodeling for Ireland, with his knob still hanging out’, hailing Uncle Stephen as a ‘fellow Gael’ then embracing him.

Dumbstruck by the tale’s coarseness and cruelty, I didn’t know where or how to look.

“Seeing as we seem to agree that Tom’s drunken Irishman act ain’t funny or clever,” my uncle thundered, “let’s also agree you’ll never encourage his paddywhackery!”

* * *

The van halted in a half-built red-brick housing estate outside Huntingdon, spraying gravel on the side of a green Portacabin. Alighting on the firm ground, I was tempted to kiss it, but my uncle was already advancing towards the Portacabin – head down, long torso leaning forward – so I shuffled through the shingle after him. Suddenly, the door was half-open and an old man’s profile appeared, his skin wrinkly and rust-colored, his thin hair wiry silver. He spat out an aniseed-scented, urine-yellow liquid, which rainbowed in the air, cascaded down, turned brown on the sandy gravel.

“Lemme guess Tom,” my uncle snapped, “Trev offered you a glass of Poteen, but it turned out to be water, and drinking that’s against your religion, so you gobbed it.”

Tom’s crumpled face tightened, like old leather being stretched; his beady hazel eyes stood out of its brown roundness. The shaving-brush bristles clung on to his head, against the breeze.

“Hold your whist! I’m only having me morning gargle.”

Tom’s accent was just like my grandmother’s; I smiled to think she’d found a way to welcome me to the site.

"This is my nephew, Charlie," my uncle said, "so mind your pints and quarts around him, and don't let me catch you expectorating intoxicants on his *501s* again."

He had to be joking – the liquid was obviously Listerine and it had fallen nowhere near me – but neither of the men were smiling. Tom opened the door fully and stepped down. He was about half my uncle's height, and easily twice his age, but his body looked sinewy beneath his spruce brown corduroy jacket and crisp cream shirt, while his glare set my heart pounding. I took a step back.

"Would it kill ye to keep your fibbing mouth shut?"

After holding my uncle's death stare, Tom turned towards me, his grimace turning into a grin, and gripped my hand in his warm, hairy paw. He smelt sweetly, of Old Spice and old tobacco.

"Tom O'Reilly. A hundred thousand welcomes!" His voice was velvety, caressing. "Rest assured, I won't hold your misfortunate kinship with Mr. high-and-mighty against you. Come in and join the entertainment."

* * *

There wasn't much entertainment during my first fortnight on site, as I struggled to achieve the stamina and speed my chores demanded. I carted Jenga towers of bricks from the store to the two bricklayers as they put up the ground floor of a semi and kept them supplied with the moldy-smelling cement Tom mixed up. During breaks, I nursed the grazes and gashes on my forearms, with hands that seemed to be wearing sandpaper gloves.

I soon learned that a skivvy's life was a sentence of hard, badly-paid labor – judging by my seventy-five-pounds-per-week wages. Still, I wasn't there to gain lucre (my parents would be paying all my university expenses) but experience and writing material. Anyway, after all the lonely months of A-level revision I'd done, it was a relief to be outside, with other workers, doing manual chores with clear procedures, and immediate deadlines; besides, I wasn't in my father's office and shadow. Another perk was returning to my parents' immaculate country bungalow, covered in grime, reeking of BO and the crew's fags. Every time she gave me a welcome-home hug, my mother held her upturned nose, and her pink face turned the color of her fading-blonde perm. At dinner, I'd offload on her gritty descriptions of my working day (my gutless father worked late, doubtless to avoid this ordeal). Afterwards, I'd dash off an entry, in a notebook journal I entitled 'My Life on the Tools'.

During week three, the brickies moved up to the first floor of the house in progress, so I tried to carry bricks up the ladder to them in a hod. Packed with a dozen slabs, the hod seemed to weigh half as much as I did. On my first attempt, I climbed halfway, slipped on a rung, and fell off, landing awkwardly, just clear of the cascading bricks.

Tom rushed over, picked me up, dusted me down. Chuckling, he proclaimed a miracle, attributing it to Saint Barbara – patron of builders and the Irish Army.

"It'd be a terrible thing if you did yourself a real mischief," he declared, "so why not hand the bricks over to meself at the ladder's foot?"

I felt guilty, and ashamed, accepting Tom's offer, but Uncle Stephen assured me that no one expected 'a scrawny nipper to hod carry' – a comment that relieved and riled me, and turned out to be wrong.

The following day I was chatting to Tom near the ladder, when an almighty 'Oi!' dropped on us from the scaffold. I looked up, into Trev's large, gap-toothed mouth, which was showering Mockney and saliva on me.

"You ain't at university yet, four eyes, so stop idling. You're here to do a man's job of work."

His shaven, football-shaped head jerked, his red jowls and beer gut wobbled, but his chest was taut under his white Three Lions T-shirt, and his arms bulged as he gripped the top rail.

"If you ain't man enough to do your duties, stick insect, at least don't put that Paddy smurf off doing his. He don't need any more excuses to slummock. So stuff your ponytail in your gob and get cracking."

As Trev stomped off, the scaffold planks trembled; so did my legs. Tom put his left arm round me and raised his right fist at the hulking retreating figure.

"It's 'serf' ye half-thick, quarter-civilized blackguard. Now ye Limeys can't butcher anyone else's language you're setting about your own! As for the young fella, he's doing a grand job altogether, so subdue your noise or you'll get what's what."

I tried to smile my thanks at Tom, with quivering lips, while looking around for my uncle, whom I eventually spotted strutting to the store, shaking his head.

* * *

At break time in the snot-green canteen, after a fast-food binge and endless fags, Trev would let off wind from both ends then kip, while my uncle scrutinized the *Times* or catnapped. Whenever the others slept, Tom stirred up the Portacabin's fuggy, fusty atmosphere with songs about the hard life of Irish immigrants on the tools in imperial England and reminiscences of the 'good old country'. For reasons still unclear to me, my uncle had made me promise not to encourage Tom's 'Paddywackery', but that couldn't have been a boycott on his company, surely. If he ever caught us gassing, I'd say I was lending Tom an ear, in exchange for the hand he was giving me on site.

But the truth was, I'd fallen headlong in love with Tom's way with – and of running away with – words. His language seemed so much more alive (alive, O!) than the stiff, pretentious English I'd been forced to regurgitate in my A-level essays, and the snobbish BBC-ese my parents encouraged me to imitate. Tom's witty phrases, and invocations of obscure saints, lit up my diary entries, and recalled my grandmother's talk. His sudden outbursts on what he called Ireland's 'English Question' could have come from the plays of O'Casey. Not that Tom seemed at all 'stagey' to me – in fact, the more I got to know him, the more I suspected my uncle was the faker. His account of the laborer's crude exhibition at the hotel now appeared unbelievable, or believable only if the courteous and cultured laborer had one of those evil twins who appeared in Irish mythology.

Often, Tom told anecdotes about everyday episodes in a rambling, humorous style. They would begin with a wink and an outrageous claim – "*The Shannon Stallion* came in for me at 45-to-1, swaggered over the finishing line." His exaggerations then spiraled like the smoke that rose from his full-strength, full-time, *Capstan* cigarettes – "That makes six winners this week. Which is just as well, and me about to buy a princely plot in Limerick for me retirement." After each embellishment he'd let out a machine-gun cackle, which usually turned into a violent cough, while I roared.

One lunchtime we were so raucous we woke my uncle, who got up, strode over.

"While I'm at *Wickes*, Charles Oliver, get the store shipshape. And start instanter – never mind about leaving Tom to blarney away to himself – he's used to it."

As Uncle Stephen marched to the door, Tom shouted.

"Ye seem very unpopular with yourself today, and 'tisn't hard to see why. Yer talk's a disgrace to the nation."

I made to follow my uncle, but stopped when Tom muttered:

"Charles Oliver? Charles Oliver! Now, there's a double-barrel made in England to put the heart crossways inside an Irishman."

"I hate the names my father gave me."

"May the curse of Cromwell be upon him – that handle's a holy terror."

"I hope my Irish ancestry and Catholic upbringing atone for it and even qualify me as Anglo-Irish."

"Kinship with Brigid Gallagher makes you as Irish as Cú Chulainn, never mind 'Anglo-Irish', which means a Protestant on a horse. Didn't I often talk to your grandmother at mass, and at O'Brien's after? This calls for a celebration, my darling! Sit down and take your ease."

As Tom skipped outside, I sat down but didn't feel easy, even though Trevor was snoring loudly. I became edgier still when Tom returned brandishing a large bottle of Guinness and poured the liquid licorice into two greasy tumblers.

"Whoa there, Tom – I don't drink – and Commander Killjoy over there might wake up – and my uncle might return anytime. You know he abominates booze."

"That teetotalitarian's the abomination! Not that I touch the drink on the tools meself, as a golden rule. Still, 'twould be sinful not to toast the Dark Rosaleen [i.e. Ireland] and your grandmother's memory."

He downed his drink in one, then nodded at mine.

"Put a hole in that."

I'd never drunk alcohol before, and was in no hurry to start, especially on a job my abstinent uncle had given me as a favor. Yet I couldn't offend Tom, or Ireland, or my grandmother, so I raised a shaky glass to them, and to convivial working-class culture, then tried to carry it to my lips. Some beer spilt over the trembling brim, but I managed a frothy sip. The acidic liquid hit my stomach hard. I let out a whistle, which morphed into a sigh as a warm numbness flooded my body and brain. Tom refilled his glass, then raised it, laughing.

"To your good health and Ireland's – to the restoration of the sick counties."

I joined in the toast, without understanding it, then sat there, beaming, as he encouraged me through my 'First Pint rite'. Yet I was sad that job had been left to Tom – wasn't it a father's or an uncle's responsibility?

Tidying the store legless was great craic, though it took time, because of my booze-fingers, and all the empty Jameson and Guinness bottles I found under the floorboards (there were some full ones too). Heading home that evening, the soft feelings generated by the stout hardened into a headache, which was aggravated by my uncle's daredevil-may-care driving. To take my thoughts of both, I asked the first thing that came to my head.

"What are the sick counties?"

His fag smoke went down the wrong way.

"Sick counties?" he spluttered, "Sick-to-death-of-death counties, more like ... It's how Tom refers to Northern Ireland, because he *never* refers to 'Northern Ireland', to avoid acknowledging it's part of the Evil Empire he pet hates (except when it offers work or benefits). He's a Rome-Rule Republican, a united-Ireland firebrand, who gawps at the butchery through emerald glasses, from a safe distance. So keep yours, you well-oiled eejit."

I sat in appalled and guilty silence all the way home. Later, however, while writing my journal, I consoled myself with the thought that Tom had uttered the toast tongue-in-cheekily, and by recalling my uncle's bizarre habit of exaggerating, or inventing, Tom's defects.

* * *

Speeding to work in mid-July, my uncle waved around an imaginary wad of banknotes:

"I've bagged a new job for the dastardly, motley crew – sixteen semis in Cambridge – and I'll be upgraded to foreman for the duration, which means '*loadsa money*'! Easily enough to enrol on the surveying course that'll be my escape to victory."

He puffed an invisible cigar, Gordon-Gekko style.

"Hereafter, I'll be spending most breaks away from the dinosaurs' graveyard [i.e. the canteen], chinwagging with the Cambridge contractors from the call box-Tardis that's gonna transport me to a brighter future."

It was lucky Big Brother was no longer around most lunchtimes, because Tom really got into his stride as a storyteller. He recounted the construction swindles he'd pulled off, including some fantastic industrial injury claims, and a ploy for drawing the salaries of imaginary workmates. Over dinner, I relayed these tales to my mother, who'd known Tom as a child, in the hope of scandalizing her. But *I* was scandalized to discover she could overlook their outrageousness and roughness, and, eventually, even find them funny, and "almost as good as your grandmother's tall stories." Some tales were too scandalous to repeat to her, however – Tom described how he'd seduced "all the mots of my English bosses, without the eejits twigging." When I raised an eyebrow at that 'all' he shrugged.

"Sure, they were only flesh and blood. In the flower of youth, I had a fine head of Porter-black hair, muscles that stood out like ropes, and was six foot five – God's truth, it's been chronicled."

I was still a virgin, full of angst and ignorance about sex, after my repressive Catholic upbringing and my prudish father's failure to compensate for it. Women seemed as remote as the statue of Our Lady of Knock I'd used to pray to after confession. Sex was a sorrowful mystery to me, but Tom's stories took some of the sorrow and mysteriousness out of it.

Yet, even during the word-feasts Tom served up at lunch, I couldn't forget the poverty of his mornings after. Slouching in the canteen at six, he'd stare vacantly into vacancy, his gaunt face fag-ash gray. But while his hangovers clung on until mid-morning, by lunchtime they'd let go miraculously, and he'd declare himself 'able for storytelling'.

One lunchtime, over a shared Guinness, while Tom was telling me a tale about a Mother Superior in his old Limerick parish, who'd trafficked illegitimate children to rich American adopters for cash – "Why, it's enough to make you renounce your religion, if not your faith; sure, don't you go to heaven in spite of the nuns and priests?" – I felt a shadow cast over me, and turned to see my uncle, whose early return from the Tardis I hadn't expected or noticed. He glared at my glass, then shook his head.

During our helter-skelter drive home that evening, he thundered at me through cigarette smoke.

"Did I, or did I not, ask you not to encourage Tom's Paddy act? Yet there you are, prompting his half-cut, quarter-true stories. It's gone so far, it's gone off. Don't mistake the University-of-Life experience I've given you for your real life, which will begin at university. And don't bystand too close to a soaked, sputtering squib like Tom – another centimeter and you'll get scorched."

I was stunned by the sharpness of his criticisms – and the concern that must have prompted them. He inhaled loudly through his nose, which was his way of signaling that a discussion had ended. But I wanted to take a debate with him into extra time, for the first time, even though I couldn't think of much to say.

"Maybe I'm wrong but, Tom seems like a good influence ... almost a father figure."

"Because he plies you with blarney and booze?"

I knew he was right, but again came the urge to answer back:

"Maybe all his stories aren't all true, but then neither are yours. That tale about his knob was fantasy, or a nightmare maybe." He scowled, then shrugged.

Smiling at my little victory, I ploughed on.

"And Tom's not stage Irish at all – he's as authentic as gran – and often reminds me of her, actually."

He banged down his fist on the dashboard.

"Have you gone queer in the head?"

"I meant in a generational ... in a historical ... ."

"Sure, they were both forced to leave the failed Irish state and join the Irish welfare-staters here, but while she helped build the 'British' welfare state, through care work, Tom only scabs off, and slanders, it. Can you imagine what it was like for me growing up in a Little Ireland populated with Toms, and presided over by whiskey priests? You can't – you're from another class, country, world – the kind of place I'm gonna get to."

I sat, shoulders slumped, gawping at the motorway catseyes. His words were unanswerable, but not unquestionable. They seemed to echo the 'better yourself' propaganda of my parents, which I'd come to the site to escape. If my uncle was on their side, there was no point arguing with him. Also, they were further evidence of his oddly intense relationship with Tom, which I still couldn't fathom. These thoughts gave me some distance from my drubbing and emboldened to demonstrate that he hadn't crushed me entirely.

"How are Tom's stories "half-cut"? Surely it's the morning's that abstinence that sobers him up."

"Tom doesn't dry out – he irrigates, lubricates. Who turned the store into a bottle graveyard? Why d'you think I asked you to tidy it? And here endeth another lesson from life's university."

* * *

A fortnight later, at lunch, Tom and I had the canteen to ourselves. My uncle was 'down the Tardis', Trev was sprawled out asleep on the table, his fat tongue lolling out, and a soggy J-cloth clasped in his hand, with water pooling around both.

"The three of us were in this shebeen," Tom tittered, "slinging pints into ourselves, when this pinched fella comes in with a spade and coal scuttle and fecks the burning fire from the grate, then scarpers. And would you credit it – the landlord charges me with the filching, on account of me 'suspect' accent. So your uncle and I stood up for Ireland and beat the backside off the bigot .... ."

Out of the corner of my eye I saw something blue flying towards us; instinctively, I moved my head back – a J-cloth whizzed past my nose and struck Tom's face with a splat, made a surprised-skull mask, then peeled off and flopped to the table.

"Jesus, Mary, and Holy St. Joseph!"

"That's enough Paddy bollocks." Trev yawned, "You couldn't stand that night, let alone stand up for Ireland, and what would Lord Snooty Sober have been doing drinking with riff-chaff like us?"

"Is it gone queer in the head ye are?"

Jumping up, like a Jack tar out of a box, Trev bellowed.

"If you're calling me queer, I'll nut you all the way to that cattle boat you come over on, and you can piss off home. Makes sense herding you with livestock – you Micks are full of bull, and your Bridgets are all dirty cows."

Tom jumped up, faster than a hare.

"Go get a mass said for the repose of your soul, or you'll die roaring for a priest. Our women live like nuns!"

I dived under the table, then gaped up at Tom – his face was traffic-light red, his mouth all fangs and froth, his fists tightening into wrecking balls. A wave of nausea rose from my stomach, broke in a series of burps, as I watched him effing and puffing.

Trev lurched round to Tom, and raised his right arm high, as though it were a truncheon.

"You'll bring on a Sean Connery, getting narky at your age Paddy; so act it, or I'll batter you, *again*."

Paling, Tom swayed, as though hit, though Trev was lowering his fist.

"Don't fancy getting the boat back? Don't blame you – ain't no construction work in your third-world country is there. All you do is blow up stuff we built so you wouldn't have to live in bogs – and that's the thanks we get for civ ... civiliz ... for giving you fucking civilization out of the cockles of our hearts."

"Ye know feck all about anything ... ," Tom screeched, "we built round towers for our saints and scholars when yees were living *outside* of caves ... God and his blessed mother ... I don't have the wind for it ... ."

Then he staggered outside, muttering.

"Ballocks to the lot of yees!"

Trev opened his arms, sang "No surrender, to the IRA" after Tom, then glared down at me.

"Air raid's over, bunker boy, so get up, and go change your knickers, then get out and on with it."

After I scrambled to my feet, he grabbed my shoulder, sprayed spit and words into my face.

"You're a bigger disgrace than the Anglo-Irish Agreement, you Paddy-loving traitor; Maggie ought to bring back National Service, sort you out. *I'll* be sorting you out, if you egg on Shameless O'Sluggard again."

* * *

All afternoon, my head throbbed with the echo of Trev's threats, while the memory of Tom's transformation into the big bad wolf sickened me, and his parting words stung me like a slap. It was one thing to listen to stories about punch ups in patriotic causes, quite another to participate in one. While I'd admired Tom's defense of Ireland, my instinct had been to back off. I felt ashamed but knew my instinct was right. I had to admit that my self-righteous uncle had been right also – being close to Tom had brought me too close to trouble and made me lose my bearings on site.

The following dawn, Tom looked like death lukewarmed up. Slumped in the canteen, he nodded at the tea my uncle gave him, before nodding off. Then his face contorted with pain, and he started sleep-talking, or shouting.

"You're away with fairies and furies, Tom!" My uncle cried, "Subdue your noise now." When that failed to rouse Tom into quiet semi-consciousness, Uncle Stephen went over and shook him gently.

That morning Trev fired a barrage of insults and orders at Tom, who'd take a step back, whistle, then return to his work. After lunch, however, Trev yelled one curse too many, and Tom screamed back.

"Give over or I'll give you a good clatter on the gob!"

"That mean you wanna go toe-to-toe bog-breath?" Trev gripped Tom's throat until the veins bulged; Tom froze, then seemed to slacken and shrivel; "Well, shut it then Murphy and behave!"

And Tom did 'behave' until the following day, when Trev sang a song about the protruding ribs of the IRA hunger-striker Bobby Sands, and the whole Punch-and-Judy show started up, and ended the same way, though this time when Trev grabbed Tom's throat, I saw my uncle clench his trowel, and release it only when Trev let Tom go.

On the journey home that day, I tried to kindle my uncle's nascent sympathy for Tom, by remarking that Trev's racism must be typical of all the discrimination Tom had surely endured since arriving in 'No dogs, no blacks, no Irish' post-war England. "*You* don't need to tell *me* about 'Murphy-bashing'" my uncle answered icily, before claiming that Tom had 'Irish Lorded' it over Trev when the latter had been 'fresh out of borstal', and that it was only after the Irish bully had hit fifty, and all the hangovers, and the hours skivvying had caught up with him, that Trev had started getting his own back, and eventually battered Tom into his 'current pitiful, self-pitying, stage-Irish mode'. So, despite their superficial differences – "Paddy and Mr Punch; the Irish Bull and the Johnny Bullshit" – the two men were "the same building-site thug, just at different stages of the bully life cycle."

Even if my uncle's history were true, it lacked historical context, and I told him as much, and much more, accusing him of ignoring history, on purpose, for his own purposes. He didn't reply, either because he couldn't, or felt he didn't need to. After hearing about Tom's strongman years and alcoholism, and witnessing his impotent explosions, and feeling the sharpness of his tongue, I no longer saw him through emerald spectacles. To keep out of harm's way, I steered clear of him, though safety came at a price. Without his canteen table talk, or the illusion of camaraderie to sustain me, I struggled to get through the back-breaking work sessions. I no longer had much to write at home about either, so I read my previous diary entries instead. I was delighted to see how my once stiff English had limbered up, through contact with Tom's and Uncle Stephen's talk, but sad to think my journal, and my adventure, were over. Gradually, if guiltily, I started to look forward to leaving the site in September and starting university.

One August evening my mother asked for one of Tom's tall tales; when I told her I didn't have any more, she said she was sorry, for both of us. She then said she and my father were sorry for having arranged the summer placement at the solicitor's without asking me – they'd only done what they'd thought best, would I forgive them? I said I'd think about it, but tried not to, for fear I'd end up thinking an office would have been a better place for me to work after all. While it never came to that, I did start to accept that I came from Middle England, rather than my grandmother's lower-class world of Irish songs and stories, and belonged there, or at any rate, couldn't leave.

* * *

On my last afternoon on site, as I was tidying the store, Tom brought me a cuppa.

"Pour some nourishment into yourself." He chortled, lacing the steaming liquid with whiskey from a small *Jameson* bottle he fished out of his jacket pocket. "Irish tay!"

After drinking from the whiskey bottle, he took my hand and shook it, with a hand shaking so much I didn't know where his shakes ended, and our shake began.

"All honor and power to you and your studies, Charlie. The Lord be between you and all harm. And, when the time comes, say a prayer for me – to Saint Jude."

* * *

That autumn I began life as well as university, discovering sex, drugs and the wider world of booze, outside of Irish bevvies; I also wrote a play for pub theatre. In it, a laborer from Limerick told stories to himself to get through his crucifying day at work. I wanted to prove to my uncle that Tom's tales were a class of literature, and to my parents that laboring had been beneficial for my writing career. Not that my relationship with my parents was difficult any longer. Mum sent me long letters, mostly about her embattled immigrant childhood and my grandmother; my father posted generous cheques. I was overjoyed to spot mum and Uncle Stephen in the audience on my play's last night, and to hear her compliments afterwards. "Your grandmother would be proud – of herself as well as you. Half the words were hers!" Uncle Motormouth said nothing about the play – which I regarded as the highest form of praise – and from backstage I'd spotted him laughing.

That was the only time I met him during the 1988-89 academic year, which turned out to be a terrible period for his crew. The housing market collapsed in October, when interest rates went double-digit. The 'loadsamoney' project he'd lined up in Cambridge was pulled. He'd found piecemeal work for the crew until spring, but wages became so awful he'd been forced to lay off Tom.

"It's survival of the shape-shiftiest;" he told me, over the phone in April, "T. Rex Trev will soon follow Tom to extinction, while I'm gonna make the evolutionary leap. I'm putting down the tools for good – very – and going to stack shelves in *Tesco's*. Then I'll bet my pittance, plus a loan from a shark, on a surveying course at the IOU."

In May, I called to see how he was doing ("fine, dandy") and asked how Tom was.

"The bottle's hit him and he's going to pieces. He's a wilderness-years George Best, without the alcohol-flashbacks to the glory days. Since he always worked on the lump, he doesn't qualify for Maggie's minimalist benefits. So he nostalgia tours the pubs, telling tall hard-luck tales, to bum drinks off English patronizers. It's game, set, and drinking match over. If he went home, his relatives would ask why he'd stopped sending money, and 'when are you going back?' His end is well-nigh; it can't come quickly enough."

I guessed he was exaggerating but couldn't be sure Tom wasn't really 'at the edge of the end', so I called my uncle again a week later for an update. He told me Tom was dead. For a minute, all I could hear was his heavy breathing on the line. A half-forgotten prayer to Jude, the patron of lost causes, came to my lips, but it was interrupted by my uncle's laughter.

"According to the nurse at the hospice, Tom's dying words were aimed at Father Pat, who tried to wangle a devout a death-bed confession out of him – 'What are ye here for?' Tom screamed at the priest, 'Is it burying me alive ye want to be? How could I be dying, when ye know better than anyone that ye can't kill a bad thing.'"

My uncle delivered the line with relish, in perfect-pitch imitation.

"Yet after the funeral, down O'Brien's, the whiskey priest assured us Tom had put on a grand play act of contrition at the last. 'And it's how you die that matters boys,' says he, to the mainly female company, which included your mother, 'not how you live.' So it was odds-on Tom was up there, he said, in the snazzy version of O'Brien's they've got in heaven, enjoying the perpetual life of O'Reilly to come. However, I don't think Tom's story should be given a happy-ever-after ending, do you?"

Author's note

I don't think Tom's story should be given a happy ending, let alone a 'happy-ever-after' one. That would belittle the hardships of the first-generation Irish immigrants I knew, back in the 1980s, who were models for the character of Tom. However, there was a happier ending for the second-generationers on whom the characters of the uncle and mother were loosely based; the pair in question now have no difficulty acknowledging their Irish ancestry and identity, and have acquired Irish Citizenship. As for the third-generationer on whom the narrator is based – well, that was me, and I recently obtained Irish citizenship too. It was, in fact, the process of applying for an Irish passport, and all the memories and meditations that churned up, which prompted this story. 'Anglo-Irish' is dedicated to the person through whom I was able to acquire Irish citizenship – my grandmother, Mary Bridget Fanning, née Danaher (born Glenagower, Ireland, 1927, died St. Neots, England, 2019), Requiescat in Pace. Thanks to Dr. David Clare (University of Limerick) for his advice about Limerick Irish-English.

www.ingramcontent.com/pod-product-compliance
Lightning Source LLC
LaVergne TN
LVHW051001080826
845145LV00009B/2394

* 9 7 8 2 3 9 0 6 9 0 6 0 3 *